THE CHILDREN ACT

IAN MCEWAN

LEVEL

RETOLD BY ANNA TREWIN
SERIES EDITOR: SORREL PITTS

PENGUIN BOOKS

UK | USA | Canada | Ireland | Australia
India | New Zealand | South Africa

Penguin Books is part of the Penguin Random House group of companies
whose addresses can be found at global.penguinrandomhouse.com.

www.penguin.co.uk   www.puffin.co.uk   www.ladybird.co.uk

The Children Act first published by Vintage Books, 2014
This Penguin Readers edition published by Penguin Books Ltd, 2021
001

Original text written by Ian McEwan
Text for Penguin Readers edition adapted by Anna Trewin
Original copyright © Ian McEwan, 2014
Ian McEwan is an unlimited company registered in England and Wales no 7473219
Text copyright © Penguin Books Ltd, 2021
Cover image copyright © Entertainment One Ltd. 2017

Set in 11/16 pt Baskerville
Typeset by Jouve (UK), Milton Keynes
Printed and bound in Great Britain by Clays Ltd, Elcograf S.p.A.

The authorized representative in the EEA is Penguin Random House Ireland,
Morrison Chambers, 32 Nassau Street, Dublin D02 YH68

A CIP catalogue record for this book is available from the British Library

ISBN: 978-0-241-52081-9

All correspondence to:
Penguin Books
Penguin Random House Children's
One Embassy Gardens, 8 Viaduct Gardens,
London SW11 7BW

Contents

Note about the story

Ian McEwan is an English novelist. He has written many best-selling books, including *On Chesil Beach, Enduring Love, Saturday* and *Atonement.*

The Children Act is about Fiona Maye, who is a High Court judge, and her meeting with Adam Henry, a desperately ill boy who refuses a blood **transfusion*** because of his religion.

High Court judges deal with many complicated **cases** in court. They usually work in London, at the Royal Courts of **Justice**, but sometimes have to travel to other courts around the country. This is called going on "circuit". Fiona works in the High Court for the Family **Division** – she hears about the problems that families have, like separation and divorce. A court with more power than the High Court is the Court of Appeal, which sometimes makes the final **judgment** in a case. The most important person in English law is the Lord Chief Justice.

The lives of High Court judges are very comfortable. In court, female judges are usually called "My Lady". Fiona lives in a large apartment in a very expensive part of central London near the Royal Courts of Justice. She plays piano, eats in expensive restaurants, drinks fine wines and listens to music by pianists such as Bach and Schubert. Although she makes judgments about people who have difficult lives, her own life has been quite easy and has very little **risk** in it.

Adam is a Jehovah's Witness. Jehovah's Witnesses read the Bible – the same book that other Christians read – but they believe that **Satan** is in control of life on earth now. They believe that Jehovah (God) will one day come and destroy all people who do not share their **faith**, creating a wonderful world full of Witnesses. After Jehovah comes, the Jehovah's Witnesses say, the dead can return to this wonderful "**heaven**" on earth.

The title of the book comes from the Children Act, which was passed by the British Government in 1989. The Act decided that, in all court cases involving children, the **interests** of the children should come first.

Before-reading questions

1 Have you ever watched a court case? Write the names of the jobs of the different people who work in a court.

2 Look at the words on page 7, which are taken from the Children Act (1989). Then look online. What is the Children Act, and which country does it belong to? What do the words mean, do you think? Do you agree with them?

3 In the story, Adam's parents will not allow him to receive blood because it is against their religious beliefs, even though Adam might die without it. Have you read any other stories like Adam's, where a doctor or judge has had to make a difficult decision?

4 Fiona Maye, a High Court judge, puts her work before having children. Is it ever easy for a woman to have both children and a successful career, or must one always come before the other?

When a court determines any question with respect to . . .
the upbringing of a child . . . the child's welfare shall
be the court's paramount consideration.

Section 1(a), the Children Act (1989)

CHAPTER ONE
A declaration

London. A Sunday evening in early June. Fiona Maye, a High Court judge, was sitting back on a **chaise longue** at home, staring over her feet at the far end of the room. There, by the tall window, stood a bookcase, and on its far side, the fireplace, which had not been lit in more than a year. Next to the window, hung a small painting by Renoir, which she had paid fifty pounds for over thirty years ago. It was probably not a real Renoir. Below it, on a round wooden table, stood a blue vase. She could not remember how she had got it, nor when she had last put flowers in it. A large shiny piano stood in the corner of the room with family photographs on top of it. And on the floor next to her was the **draft** of a **judgment**.

In Fiona's hand was her second **whisky** and water. She was feeling shaky, still recovering from a bad moment with her husband. She did not often drink, but today it was helping her to feel calmer, and she thought about getting herself a third. But less whisky and more water this time because she was in court tomorrow, and she was duty judge now — she had to be available for any sudden demand, even as she lay recovering.

Her husband had made a shocking **declaration** and put an impossible weight on her shoulders. For the first time in years, she had actually shouted. "You **idiot!** You **bloody** fool!" She had not **sworn** since visiting her cousins in Newcastle when she was young.

And then she'd said, "How could you ask that?" but he'd answered calmly, "I need it. I'm fifty-nine. This is my last chance. I've not yet heard **evidence** about an afterlife."

She'd simply stared at him, lost for a reply. Finally, she'd said, "Jack, this is too crazy."

"Fiona, when did we last have sex?"

When did they? He had asked this before, although not in this kind of mood, but the recent past had been so busy that it was difficult to remember. The Family **Division** of the court was full of strange differences, special demands, half-truths and half-lies, and angry **accusations**. All the information had to be collected and understood speedily. Last week, Fiona had heard final **submissions** by the lawyers of divorcing **Jewish** parents about the education of their two daughters. The draft of her finished judgment lay on the floor beside her.

And then tomorrow, coming before her again in court, would be a different **case**. A mother, an English woman, thin, pale, highly educated. She was the mother of a five-year-old child who she was sure was about to be taken out of the country by the father, a Moroccan businessman and strict Muslim, to a new life in Rabat. After that, there would be the usual accusations and arguments over **residence** of children, houses and money. Parents soon learned the new vocabulary of the law and were amazed to find themselves in an angry war with the person that they used to love. And waiting away from the stage, boys and girls, worried little Bens and Sarahs, standing close together while the gods above them fought to the end. From the Family Court, to the High Court, to the Court of Appeal.

There was a sadness to all of it, but it continued to interest Fiona. She felt that she brought **reasonableness** to hopeless situations, and generally, she believed in family law. She thought it was a mark of human progress that the child's **interests** were now put above its parents'. Her days were full, and recently, her evenings had been, too. Lots of dinners, a concert at Kings Place (Schubert), taxis, tube trains, a letter to draft about a special school for the cleaning lady's son who had learning difficulties, and finally sleep.

Where *was* the sex? At that moment, she couldn't remember.

"I don't keep a record," she replied, finally.

He spread his hands – she had proved his case.

She'd watched as Jack crossed the room and poured himself some whisky. Recently, he'd been looking taller, easier in his movements. When he turned his back to her, she felt the possibility of his rejection; she would be **humiliated** by being left for a younger woman. Of being left, useless and alone. She wondered if she should simply agree to anything he wanted, then quickly rejected the thought.

He'd come back towards her with his glass. He did not offer her a drink the way he usually did around this time.

"What do you want, Jack?" she asked.

"I'm going to have this **affair**."

"You want a divorce."

"No, I want everything to be the same. No lies."

"I don't understand."

"Yes, you do. Didn't you once tell me that couples in long marriages become like brothers and sisters? That's us, Fiona.

11

We've arrived. It's comfortable and sweet, and I love you, but before I drop dead, I want one big **passionate** affair."

She breathed in hard, and he must have thought that she was laughing. "**Ecstasy**," he said, angrily. "Remember that? Almost fainting with the **thrill** of it. I want to do it one last time, even if you don't. Or perhaps you do."

This was when she had found her voice. She swore at him again and told him how stupid he was. She had a strong hold on what was meant to be right. That he had, she knew, always been **faithful**, made this suggestion even more crazy. Or if he'd been unfaithful in the past, he'd hidden it brilliantly. She already knew the name of the woman. Melanie. She knew that she could be destroyed by this affair with this twenty-eight-year-old **statistician**, who worked with him at the university where he was a **professor** of History.

"If you do this, it will be the end for us," she had said. "It's as simple as that."

"Is this a **threat**?" he asked.

"No, it's a promise."

By now, she was angry again. And it did seem simple. The moment to make this declaration about wanting an open marriage was before the wedding, not thirty-five years later. To **threaten** everything they had so that he might relive a small thrill? When she tried to imagine doing something like that herself, she could only think of trouble, secret meetings, disappointment. Then the necessary separation from that person, and nothing would be the same when she came away. No, she preferred an imperfect life, the one she had now.

But sitting here now on the chaise longue, she realized how awful the insult had been. How he was prepared to pay for his thrills with her unhappiness. She had seen him be determined in the past, but this was new. What had changed? He stood tall in front of her as he poured his whisky, his free hand moving as if he was listening to a tune inside his head. Some shared song perhaps, but not shared with her. Hurting her and not caring – that was new. He had always been kind, and kindness, the Family Division had shown her, was the most important human quality. As a judge, she, Fiona, was able to remove a child from its parents, and she sometimes did. But to remove herself from an unkind husband? When she was weak and sad? Where was her own judge to offer her protection?

Self-pity in others embarrassed her, and she didn't want to feel it now. She would have a third drink instead. But she only poured herself a small amount of whisky, and put a lot of water in it. Then, she returned to the chaise longue. Yes, it had been the kind of conversation for which she should have taken notes. It was important to remember each insult. When she threatened to end the marriage if he had the affair, he had just repeated himself. He had told her again how much he loved her and always would, that there was no other life than this. But his un-met **sexual** needs were causing him great unhappiness. There was this one chance, and he wanted to take it, but he wanted her to know about it and to give him her **permission**. He said that he could have done it "behind her back". Her thin, unforgiving back.

"That's good of you, Jack," she said, coldly.

"Well actually . . ." he said, but did not finish.

13

She guessed that he was about to tell her that the affair had already begun, but she could not bear to hear it. She did not need to. She could see it. A pretty statistician hoping that he would stop wanting to come home to his angry, unhappy wife. A sunny morning, a strange bathroom, Jack pulling a clean shirt over his head in that way he had, and another shirt being thrown towards the washing basket. It would happen, with or without her permission.

"The answer's no," she said, simply. Then she'd added, "What else do you expect me to say?"

She felt helpless and wanted the conversation to end. She'd already made her judgment in the case of the two Jewish schoolgirls, but she needed to read through it one more time to check for any small mistakes. Outside, the summer rain beat against the windows, and she could hear wet car tyres below their apartment on Gray's Inn Square. He would leave her, and the world would go on.

His face had been tight as he'd turned to leave the room. At the sight of his back she'd felt a cold fear. She would have called after him, but what could she say? "Hold me, kiss me, have the girl." She listened to his feet walking down the hall, then the sound of their bedroom door closing.

CHAPTER TWO
A phone call

First the facts. Both parents were from the strict **Chareidi** Jewish **community** in North London. The Bernsteins' marriage had been arranged by their parents. Thirteen years later, the couple were now separated. Their two children, Rachel and Nora, lived with the mother but had a lot of contact with the father. After the difficult birth of the second child, the mother was not able to have any more babies. The father wanted a large family, and so the marriage began to fail. After being **depressed** (for a short time, she said, for a long time, he said), the mother did a university course and became a primary school teacher. The many relatives were not happy about this because in the Chareidi community, women were not expected to work. They were meant to raise children and look after the home. So the family wanted the girls to live with their father.

Chareidi men did not get much education either. They did not usually go to university and were expected to spend most of their time studying the **Torah**. Chareidi boys and girls were not allowed fashionable clothes, television or the internet, and they were educated separately. But the mother had already sent the girls to a mixed boys and girls Jewish school where non-Jewish children also studied. She wanted them to stay there and go on to university. She planned for them to have the chances in life that she'd never had and be able to earn their own money when they were adults. University would allow them to meet men who earned money and could help to support a family, she'd decided. Unlike her husband, who gave all his time to studying and teaching the Torah for eight hours a week, without pay.

Mr Bernstein's lawyer argued that Judith Bernstein was a selfish woman who could not separate her interests from her children's. What she said they needed was what she really wanted for herself. She was taking the girls away from a safe and happy home, strict but loving, with clear rules. Members of the Chareidi were generally happier than people from the world outside, his lawyer said.

Fiona looked up from checking the draft for a moment. No sound from the bedroom. Just the traffic and the rain. Fiona hated the way that she was listening out for him. The sound of a door or a step on the wooden floor. Wanting it, not wanting it.

Fiona had made her judgment. She was known for being understanding, **reasonable** and highly intelligent. The Lord Chief Justice was even heard to speak to a **colleague** about her as "distant and mysterious, but very understanding, and still beautiful" (although Fiona knew that she was slowly losing that beauty). She had ruled for Mrs Bernstein. The court was being asked to choose between two ways of life, she had written. She had to take a long view, remembering that a child today could live into the twenty-second century. This meant that education, the ability to work and have financial **freedom**, a large circle of friends and family and chances at work, were of most importance.

The whisky sat in the glass untouched. She had started to hate the smell of it. She should be angrier; she should be talking to one of her old friends; she should be going into the bedroom and demanding to know more. But she had to finish checking this judgment.

No child was an island, she wrote. She thought of Shakespeare's play *Antony and Cleopatra*. "Nor custom stale her infinite variety." She knew the words well because she had once spoken them when she played Enobarbus in *Antony and Cleopatra* at Oxford one sunny afternoon, not long after she had finished her law exams. Around that time, Jack had fallen in love with her, and not long after, she with him. They first made love in a borrowed room at the top of a house with a window that brought in the golden evening sun. It had a view of the Thames river.

She thought of Jack's lover, his statistician, Melanie. She had met her once; a silent young woman with a heavy necklace and stupidly high shoes. Was he **obsessed** with her? Would Melanie pull him away from home and eat him up, leaving nothing of past and future, as well as present? Or would he be back within the fortnight, his hunger over, making plans for the family holiday?

Fiona looked up and saw her husband on the other side of the room, pouring another drink. It was a big one, and he did not add water. He'd come in barefoot, so she'd not heard him. He turned and came towards her with the drink in his hand. His body still looked quite strong – he played tennis and lifted weights every day, while she did nothing except use the stairs at work instead of the lift. He was handsome in a messy way, with relaxed shoulders and bright eyes that looked for adventure.

He sat down in the nearest chair. "You couldn't answer my question, so I'll tell you," he said. "It's been seven weeks and a day. Are you really happy with that?"

She said, quietly, "Are you already having this affair? Because if you are, I'd like you to pack a bag and leave now."

He knew that a difficult question was best answered by another. "You think we're too old? Is that it?"

It troubled her to think that he might be right. They'd had a good sex life for many years, regular and easy, on weekdays in the early morning just as they woke, at weekends in the afternoons sometimes after playing tennis. It had been good for years and needed no words to describe it. It was one reason why she hated him to mention it now and had not noticed that recently they'd made love less often.

But she had always loved him, always cared for him. Only last year she had looked after him when he broke his leg in a ski race with friends in France. She had even sat on top of him during sex in a hotel room in Paris, while he lay on the bed smiling. But she did not know how to use these things in her **defence**, and she knew that this was not the reason she was being attacked. It was not her love he was questioning, it was her *passion*.

Then there was age. They were not old yet, but the beginnings of it were showing. The white hair on Jack's chest and less muscle on his body. His face was a bit thinner, and sometimes there was an emptiness in his eyes. And her own bottom getting bigger; her waist thickening and the corners of her mouth beginning to point down. This was fine in a serious-faced judge, but in a lover?

"I don't think we should give up, do you?" he said.

"You're the one who's walking away."

"I think you have a part in this, too."

"I'm not the one who's about to destroy our marriage."

"So you say." He said it reasonably, then swallowed some of his drink. "You know I love you."

"But you'd like someone younger."

"I'd like a sex life."

She looked away and said nothing. She was not going to allow him to push her into having sex with him, especially when she suspected that the affair had already begun. He had not said differently.

"Well," he said, "wouldn't you?"

"Not with this gun to my head," she replied.

"Meaning?"

"If I don't start having sex with you again, you'll go to Melanie."

She had not spoken the woman's name before. She saw his face go tight, and suddenly she felt ill. She pushed herself forward on the chaise longue, the judgment papers still in her hand.

"Well, if you were me, what would you do?" he said.

"I wouldn't start seeing a man and then ask to talk," she said. "I'd find out what was worrying you first."

"Fine," he replied. "So what *is* worrying you?"

It was the most important question, and she'd invited it, but at the moment it was making her angry, and she did not reply. Instead, she looked past him down the room to the piano, which she'd hardly played in two weeks. The photos stood on top of it in their silver frames. Both their families were there: both sets of parents, his three sisters, her two brothers, their wives and husbands, past and present. Eleven nephews and nieces, who had their own young children. She and Jack had provided nothing, no one – except for organized family holidays and birthday presents. The nieces and nephews often came to stay, too. There was a cupboard in their apartment which was full of toys and a highchair.

Seven weeks and a day. A period that began with the final stages of the **conjoined twins** case. Two baby boys lay in hospital, joined at the stomach and thighs and sharing the same body. Matthew's heart was large, but it hardly worked, so Mark's heart kept them both going. Matthew's brain was small and undeveloped, and he could not feed very well. Mark was feeding normally and doing all the "work". Without separating them, Mark's heart would soon fail, and both twins would die. Matthew was unlikely to live more than six months, and when he died, he would take his brother with him. The doctors at the hospital wanted to do an **operation** that would save Mark, the strongest twin, but would sadly result in Matthew's death. The loving, very religious parents refused to allow murder. God gave life, and only God could take it away.

Everyone had something to say. Doctors, journalists, men and women on the radio, taxi drivers, relatives, people across the country. Life, love, death and a race against time. It was science against religion. Fiona found, in just under a week and in thirteen thousand words, a way forward. Separating the twins would kill Matthew, she said, but not separating them would kill both. Even if Matthew could live, it would not be for very long. It was a difficult part of the law because Fiona could make no decision to kill, so she argued that one child saved was better than two dead. The purpose of the operation was not to kill Matthew but to save Mark. Matthew would die after the operation not because he was

murdered, but because he could not survive alone. The twins
must be separated.

Most people agreed with her decision. Two days later, the
twins had their operation. For Mark it was successful, and he
lived, and people slowly lost interest in the case. But Fiona was
unhappy and could not forget about it. She had many sleepless
nights turning over the details in her mind. At the same time, the
angry letters from the religious side began to arrive, telling her
that both children should have been left to die. Some even said
that they wanted to hurt her.

Those weeks had troubled her, and they had only just begun
to fade. But the awful photographs of the twins stayed in her
mind. She started to dislike bodies and could not look at
her own or Jack's. But how was she going to talk about this? She
could not explain why, after so many years in the law, this case
had affected her so badly. She had sent a child from the world
in thirty-four pages. For a while, some part of her had gone
cold, along with poor Matthew. The feeling had passed, but it
left a mark on her memory, even after seven weeks and a day.
She would have preferred not to have had a body, but to float in
the air instead.

———

The sound of Jack's glass landing on a table returned her to the
room. He was looking at her calmly. Even if she had known how
to tell him what was worrying her, she was in no mood for it. She
had work to do, the end of her judgment on the Jewish girls to
check. The problem was the choice her husband was making.
She was suddenly angry again.

"For the last time, Jack. Are you sleeping with her? I'll take your silence as a yes."

He stood up and walked towards the piano, then turned. "Nothing has happened. I wanted to talk to you first, I wanted –"

"Do you realize what you're about to destroy?"

"I could say the same. Something is going on, and you won't talk to me."

Let him go, a voice, her own voice, said in her thoughts. And immediately she was frightened. She could not live the rest of her life alone. Two close friends, both divorced many years ago, still hated to enter a crowded room alone. And she still loved him, though she didn't feel it now.

"Your problem," he said from the piano, "is that you never think you have to explain yourself. You've gone from me. It would be OK if I thought it wasn't for long, or I knew the reason why. So . . ."

He was starting to walk towards her when the telephone suddenly rang. Without thinking, she picked it up and heard the voice of her **clerk**, Nigel Pauling. "I'm sorry to disturb you so late, My Lady."

"It's all right. Go ahead."

"We've had a call about the Edith Cavell Hospital in Wandsworth. The hospital urgently needs to do a blood **transfusion** on a **leukaemia** patient, a boy of seventeen years. He and his parents are refusing the transfusion. The hospital would like –"

"Why are they refusing?"

"They are Jehovah's Witnesses, My Lady. The hospital wants you to rule that it will be lawful to continue with the transfusion."

She looked at her watch. Just past ten-thirty.

"How long have we got?"

"After Wednesday it will be dangerous, they're saying. Extremely dangerous."

She looked around her. Jack had already left the room. Then she said, "List it for 2 p.m. on Tuesday. Ask the hospital to tell the parents."

"I'll do it straight away."

"I'll want to know why a transfusion is necessary and hear evidence from the parents."

She put down the phone then went to the window to stare across the square, where the dark shapes of trees stood against the night sky. Street lamps created yellow circles on the pavements below them. The Sunday evening traffic was light now, and all she could hear was the last drops of rain falling among the leaves in the trees. She watched a cat move around a pool of water then disappear into a neighbour's garden.

It didn't trouble her that Jack had left the room. Their conversation had been moving towards a painful directness, and she was glad to be able to move to other people's problems. Religion again. It had its uses. Since the boy was nearly eighteen – the age when, by law, he could make his own decisions – his wishes would be very important.

On the other side of the city, this teenager stared at death for his own or his parents' **faith**. It was not her job to save him, but

23

to decide what was reasonable and lawful. She would have liked to see this boy for herself. Take herself away from her troubles at home, as well as from the courtroom, for an hour or two. The parents might be pushing him into this decision, and he could be too frightened to fight them. These days, finding out such information for yourself as a judge was very unusual. Back in the 1980s, a judge could still have spoken to the teenager alone in the hospital or at home. Now, **social workers** did the job and reported back. The old way had the human touch. Now, there was less time and more boxes to tick. The lives of children were held by computers rather than humans.

But a visit to the hospital was a silly idea, and she pushed it away. She went back to the chaise longue and read through the draft of her judgment one more time. It was done. She stood and picked up the whisky glasses, and went to the kitchen to wash them. As the warm water washed over her hands, she listened out for Jack but could hear nothing. She went back into the sitting room, and then found herself back at her position at the window.

Down in the square, not far from the water that the cat had stepped around, her husband was pulling a suitcase with one hand and holding a **briefcase** with the other. He must have taken great care in the leaving the apartment – inch by lying inch – so that she did not hear him.

He reached his car, their car, opened it and put the suitcase in the back seat. Then he got in, started the engine and drove away.

He must have packed his bag earlier in the evening, when he first went to the bedroom. But instead of feeling angry, she was only tired. If she went to bed now, she thought, she might not need to take a sleeping pill. She went back to the kitchen telling herself that she was not looking for a note on the table, where they always left each other notes. There was nothing.

She went into the bedroom and opened the wardrobe. He had taken three jackets. In the bathroom, she did not open the cupboard to see what things he had put in his washbag – she already knew enough.

She slept badly. The face of the weaker twin, Matthew, came to visit her, staring at her angrily as he had on other nights. The sisters, Rachel and Nora, were calling to her, and Jack was coming closer, telling her threateningly that she needed to do more for him in the future.

When her alarm rang at six-thirty, she sat up suddenly and, for a moment, stared without understanding at the empty side of the bed. Then, she went into the bathroom and began to prepare herself for a day in court.

CHAPTER THREE
In court

She went the usual way to the Royal Courts of **Justice**, with a briefcase in one hand and an umbrella in the other. The morning was grey and dull, and the city air felt cool against her cheeks. She nodded to the friendly doorman as she left the apartments and hoped that she did not look like a woman whose world had just turned upside down. She avoided thinking about Jack by playing a **piece** of piano music she knew in her head. She imagined herself as the pianist that she could never become, performing Bach perfectly.

Rain had fallen for most days of the summer. The trees were full of it, and the streets were wet and smooth. The cars on High Holborn were showroom shiny and clean, and the Thames river was dark brown and angry as it rose against the bridges. Everyone pushed forward along the pavements, determined and wet. By the time she got to Chancery Lane, the rain was coming down harder, driven by a cold wind. It was darker now, and a shower of drops flew from a car's wheels against her legs. She was playing a slow piece of music in her mind now, but there was no escape because it led her straight to a memory of Jack. She had learned it as a birthday present for him last April. She remembered him drinking cold white wine and shouting with joy as she'd played it, and their long kiss at the end after they'd touched their glasses together.

But then the engine of self-pity began to turn, and helplessly she remembered all the kind things that she had done for him. The list was very long. There were surprise visits to the theatre, carefully planned trips to Paris and Dubrovnik, Vienna and Rome (Jack, knowing nothing, was told to pack a small bag and passport, and meet her at the airport straight from work). And so many thoughtful presents – special boots from America, a rare bottle of whisky, books about exploring.

She felt sad then, and knew that her real anger was still ahead. She was an **abandoned** fifty-nine-year-old woman taking her first steps into the beginning of old age. She made herself think of a different piece again as she turned into the narrow road that led her to Lincoln's Inn. Over the drumming of the rain she heard Bach's gentle piano still playing in her head. The music was lovely, and she felt it had some clear human meaning, or perhaps it was just about love in its biggest, largest form, for all people. For children perhaps. Johann Sebastian Bach had twenty of them from two marriages.

She wondered then if her own childlessness was a flight from the journey she had been meant to take. Had she failed to become a woman, as her mother understood that word?

How she had come to this place was the story of a long journey of many years. A story of the idea of children appearing then pulling back, then appearing again. Of shock and sometimes worry as the years when she was able to have children went by and then were gone, and she was almost too busy to notice. After her final exams, she'd started work as a lawyer and had enjoyed some early success. It had seemed reasonable to delay having a child until her thirties. But, when those years came, they brought more difficult, important cases and more success. Jack was also not sure, arguing to wait for another year while he was teaching in Pittsburgh. At the same time, she was working a fourteen-hour day, moving deeper into family law while the idea of her own family began to disappear, despite the regular visits of nephews and nieces.

Then came talk of Fiona being made a judge. And in her forties, the worry of being an older mother and that it might cause problems for the health of their child. And then one day, when she was **sworn in** by the Lord Chief Justice, she knew that it was never going to happen. She belonged to the law.

She crossed Carey Street and walked up the steps to the Courts of Justice on the Strand, through the corridors and up the stairs until she reached her office. Nigel Pauling, quiet and always correct, was **leaning** over her desk and putting out documents. They asked about each other's weekends, and she said that hers was "quiet" as she gave him the corrected draft of the Bernstein judgment. They talked about the day's cases. In the Moroccan case, listed for 10 o'clock, she learned that the little girl had been taken to Rabat by the father despite his promises to the court. The mother, who was very upset, would be in court today and Fiona would apply through the **Hague Convention** to get the child returned as soon as possible.

The papers for the Jehovah's Witness case were on her desk. The boy had a very rare type of leukaemia, Pauling told her.

"Let's give him a name," she said, sharply, and her voice surprised her.

"Of course, My Lady. Adam. Adam Henry," Pauling replied.

"The parents are Kevin and Naomi. Mr Henry runs a small digging company. Adam is their only child."

After twenty minutes, she walked along the corridor to the coffee machine and made herself a strong cup of cappuccino from fresh beans. Then, she suddenly pulled her phone from her bag and rang a business number, giving orders for a change of lock. New keys should be delivered to her office today, Fiona said, and nowhere else. There must be a price for Jack leaving her and here it was. She would not allow him to have two addresses.

The court rose for her at 10 o'clock. She listened to the lawyer of the unhappy mother who wanted to get her daughter back. When the father's lawyer started to speak, she cut him off with her hand. "I'm surprised your face isn't red from embarrassment because of what your **client** has done," she said, quickly. When the court rose, Fiona knew that she would never see the mother again. The case would go before a Moroccan judge.

Next, she heard the case of a woman who needed money from her husband for her children ahead of their divorce. She listened, she asked questions, she ruled for the mother. At lunch, Fiona wanted to be alone. Pauling brought her sandwiches and a bar of chocolate to eat at her desk. Her phone lay under some papers. At last, she gave in and looked at it for texts or missed calls. Nothing. She told herself she didn't feel anything. She drank tea and read a newspaper for ten minutes. There was a story about the war in Syria, reports and terrible photographs. The government were killing ordinary people. An eight-year-old boy lay on a bed missing a leg.

There were more unhappy cases that afternoon. She ruled

against a woman who wanted her husband out of the family home, then listened to a man who was worried about being attacked by his ex-wife's boyfriend. Back at her desk at five forty-five, and Pauling came in to tell her that media interest in the Jehovah's Witness case was strong. Most of tomorrow morning's papers would carry the story. Then Fiona's new keys arrived in a brown envelope, opening her way to a changed life.

Half an hour later, she set off towards home, but she did not go there directly because she did not want to enter the empty apartment. She walked west on the Strand instead, then went north along Kingsway. The sky was a dark grey, and she no longer noticed the rain. The Monday traffic was lighter than usual. She turned east, crossed High Holborn, and then went west again past cafés, hairdressers and small art shops, still not wanting to return. When she passed a key-cutting shop, her heart began to race as she imagined Jack shouting at her, face-to-face under the square's dripping trees while the neighbours looked on from their windows. She knew that she was in the wrong.

But, when she finally reached the apartment, coming home wasn't so difficult. She was used to getting back before Jack, and she felt relaxed as she closed the door and went to the kitchen. She put down her bag and listened to the silence, then she went through the rooms, turning on the lights although it was only seven-thirty.

She took her papers from her briefcase and read through the next day's submissions while she made some tea. She could have phoned one of three friends, but she could not bear to explain her situation and make it real. It was too soon for sympathy or advice. Instead, she spent the evening feeling nothing. She ate cheese and biscuits, and then sat at the piano and played Bach. It made her think about a colleague of hers, Mark Berner, who sometimes played with her. He was representing the hospital in the Jehovah's Witness case the next day. The next concert they would play together was at Christmas, but she decided to practise some of the pieces now. When she finally rose, her body was stiff. In the bathroom, she swallowed a sleeping pill, and twenty minutes later she was in bed, her body folded in a troubled sleep.

CHAPTER FOUR
Adam's case

The morning passed like a thousand other mornings. Submissions quickly understood, orders given, and Fiona moving between her room and the court seeing colleagues on the way. Her mood? She knew that it had changed. Yesterday, she now decided, she had been in shock, worrying about the sympathy of her family and being embarrassed at having to explain to friends. This morning, she felt like she had lost a part of her body, she felt abandoned. She thought of Jack at his best and missed him. She missed his bare chest in the morning, and rolling into his arms when the alarm clock first sounded, feeling like a child before it sounded a second time and she stepped out of bed into an adult. She had looked at herself hard in the mirror this morning. Bits of her were smaller these days, bits of her were larger. Her bottom was heavy. Why would anyone *not* leave her?

Washing, dressing, drinking coffee, leaving a note and arranging a new key for the cleaning lady – these things helped bring her feelings under control. She looked for her husband in emails, texts and post and found nothing. His silence seemed heartless, and it shocked her. But no, she would not go to find him to beg for his return. She would wait until a certain book or shirt brought him back to the apartment, and when they spoke she would be stronger because she was on her own ground.

Nobody would ever know how bad she felt when she went through her cases that morning. At lunchtime, in her room once more, she ate a sandwich and an apple at her desk while she read through the submission for the Jehovah's Witness case. The afternoon was now cleared for it. Forty minutes later, only one clear thought came with her to Courtroom Eight: this was a matter of life and death. Her private life no longer mattered.

The two **barristers** stood before her. Acting for the hospital, her colleague and friend, Mark Berner QC. For the parents, another barrister, Leslie Grieve QC. Sitting next to him were Mr and Mrs Henry. Mr Henry was a thin man who wore a suit and tie. Mrs Henry was large and wore big glasses with red frames. Neither parent looked particularly frightened or worried.

Fiona began. "You all understand that time is very important in this matter. So please be **brief** and keep to the subject. Mr Berner."

She nodded her head towards him, and he stood. He had no hair and a large body, but she knew that his singing voice was rich and deep. Together their greatest moment had been last year when they had performed Schubert's "Der Erlkönig" at a Gray's Inn dinner for an old judge who was leaving the law.

"I will be brief, My Lady," he replied. "The Edith Cavell Hospital in Wandsworth is looking for permission from this court to treat a boy, Adam Henry, who will be eighteen in less than three months. Adam experienced sharp stomach pains on the fourteenth of May when he was playing sport at school. In the next few days, these pains became terrible. His doctor didn't know –"

"I've read the papers, Mr Berner."

"Then I think everyone agrees that Adam is suffering from a rare type of leukaemia. The hospital wants to treat him in the usual way with four **drugs**. Two of the drugs target the leukaemia **cells** directly, and the other two drugs kill anything that gets in their way. This damages the body and its ability to make red and white blood cells. So the normal thing is to do a blood transfusion while the patient is being treated. However, Adam and his parents will not permit this because, as Jehovah's Witnesses, their religion does not agree with it. They will take anything else that the hospital can offer their son, but not the transfusion."

"And what *has* been offered?"

"My Lady, only the leukaemia drugs, and the hospital does not believe that they will be enough to save him. I would like now to call Dr Rodney Carter."

Dr Rodney Carter stood and was sworn in. Tall and bent, with thick white hair, he explained about Adam's blood cell count and told them that the boy was weak and was starting to find it hard to breathe. With a blood transfusion, he could expect an eighty to ninety per cent chance of recovery, though it would have been better if they'd been able to do it earlier. Without a transfusion, the situation was extremely serious. The boy could die.

Berner spoke with a low voice. "And have you talked to your patient about what kind of death he can expect?"

Fiona knew that the parents were listening but did not stop him.

"He has no idea of how bad his death will be," Carter continued. "It will be very difficult and painful, very upsetting. Some of the nurses and doctors looking after Adam are angry. They do blood transfusions all the time. They don't understand why they can't do one on him. He will fight to breathe, a fight

34

that he will find frightening and is sure to lose. He may bleed inside his body. He may go blind. Many things may happen to him, but one thing is sure. It will be a horrible death."

"Thank you, Dr Carter."

Leslie Grieve stood up to **cross-examine**. He had silver hair and a long nose and moved easily around the courtroom. Fiona had seen him a few times, but she could not remember if he had ever stood before her in court.

Grieve said, "You do accept, Dr Carter, that freedom of choice of medical treatment is an important right of a human being?"

"I do."

"And Adam is close to being an adult as the law decides it. He is nearly eighteen – seventeen years and nine months, in fact. Isn't it true that he has said what he wants clearly and intelligently?"

"His ideas are from his parents," replied Carter. "They're not his own."

"Did you know, Dr Carter, that the World Health Organization believes that between fifteen and twenty per cent of new **AIDS cases** are caused by blood transfusions?"

"I've not had any cases of AIDS in my hospital."

"And it is possible to catch other diseases through transfusion, isn't it?"

"But it's very rare."

"It's enough to make someone pause though, isn't it, Dr Carter?"

"Pause, yes," replied Carter. "But to refuse in a case like Adam's would be wrong. He may not recover. He may go blind."

The two men continued to argue for some minutes about the **risks** of blood transfusions. Finally, Fiona interrupted them.

"How much time do we have to decide this matter, Dr Carter?" she asked.

"If I can't give the boy blood by tomorrow morning, we will be on very dangerous ground," he replied.

Kevin Henry was sworn in next. Mr Grieve asked him to talk about his difficult early life, when he was a builder. He admitted that he had been "a bit of a wild man". He had drunk too much and was awful to his wife, Naomi. Though he never hit her. The baby used to cry all night, the couple argued, and the neighbours complained. Then, one day, two polite young American men had come to visit Kevin, and slowly the couple discovered the Jehovah's Witness religion. Peace and happiness came into their lives. They began to live "the truth" and discovered the future that God had planned for humans – great joy in **heaven** on earth. They promised to spread the message of their faith, as all Jehovah's Witnesses must, and slowly they became better parents, and the baby became calmer. Kevin retrained and got a new job at a digging company. The couple fell in love all over again. To end this five-minute history, Grieve asked, "Mr Henry, will you tell the court why Adam is refusing a blood transfusion?"

Kevin Henry paused for a moment, then turned to Fiona. "You have to understand," he said, "that blood is the most important part of being human. Blood is the gift of life."

"So if blood is a gift, why is your son refusing it?" asked Grieve.

"Mixing your blood with another human's, or another animal's, is pollution. It is a rejection of God's wonderful gift."

"Do you and your wife love Adam, Mr Henry?"

"Yes. We love him." Kevin Henry said it quietly and looked at Fiona.

"And if refusing the transfusion shall lead to his death?" asked Grieve.

"He will take his place in the heaven that's to come."

"And you and your wife. How about you? You'll feel terrible, won't you?"

At this, the father could only nod, and Fiona could see that he was fighting back tears.

Then, the barrister said, "Is this Adam's decision, or is it really your own?"

"We couldn't turn him from it even if we wanted to."

For several minutes, Grieve continued to question Mr Henry, intending to show that the boy was making an independent choice. Adam had been visited by the **elders** on several occasions, and they were happy that he knew his own mind. He was prepared to die and get to the wonderful heaven that he and all other Jehovah's Witnesses believed waited for him.

Then at three-thirty, Mark Berner rose to cross-examine. He began by telling the parents of his sympathy for their son's illness and hopes for his full recovery. Hearing this, Fiona guessed that he was planning on going in hard.

Berner started by reading a long paragraph from the Bible. Then he said, "So it tells you that you cannot eat blood, but there's nothing about transfusion."

Mr Henry said, patiently, "I think you'll find that in the Greek, the original meaning is not to 'take into the body'."

"But at that time, transfusion didn't **exist**. So how could they be speaking about it?"

Kevin Henry shook his head. "It existed in the mind of God. Our elders are quite clear about it."

"These strict elders have been visiting your son every day, haven't they? They are determined that he won't change his mind," said Berner.

For the first time, Kevin Henry looked angry. He stood taller and stared at Berner. "These are good men. My son gets advice and comfort from the elders. If he didn't, he would let me know."

"Isn't it true that if he agreed to be **transfused**, he would be thrown out of the faith? The community wouldn't want him?" asked Berner.

"But it isn't going to happen," replied Henry. "He isn't going to change his mind."

"But he's still a child, Mr Henry. So it's your mind I want to change. He's afraid of being thrown out for not doing what you and the elders want. The only world he knows would turn its back on him for preferring life to a terrible death. Is that a free choice for a young man?"

Kevin Henry paused to think. For the first time, he looked over at his wife. Then he turned back to Berner. "If you spent five minutes with him, you'd realize that he's someone who knows his own mind and is able to make a decision according to his faith."

Kevin Henry then went on to explain more about the faith and its beliefs. They learned that Adam wrote poetry and that this had caused arguments in the family. Finally, Mr Henry sat down. The last person to be sworn in was the social worker, Marina Greene. Adam, she said, was highly intelligent. He knew the Bible well. He said that he was prepared to die for his faith. Then she read out a note from him.

"I'm my own man. I'm separate from my parents. Whatever my parents' ideas are, I'm deciding for myself."

Fiona asked what Mrs Greene thought the court should decide. She said her view was simple. "A child shouldn't kill himself because of religion," she replied.

———

Fiona asked for a short break before hearing closing submissions from the barristers. The court rose, and she went quickly to her room, drank a glass of water and checked her emails and texts. There were plenty of both but still nothing from Jack. It didn't seem possible that the person she knew so well could be so cruel.

So she was pleased, several minutes later, to be back in court. She listened to Berner talk about previous, similar cases. He talked about Adam's obvious intelligence, his clever way with words. He had won an important poetry competition. Adam was not yet eighteen, did not understand the terrible death that lay ahead of him, but did know that he would be thrown out of the faith if he agreed to the transfusion. The ideas of Jehovah's Witnesses lay outside those of a reasonable parent.

Grieve then rose and argued that Adam was so near to eighteen that it made no difference. He was old enough to decide how he wanted to be treated. The court should take no view on a particular religion, and to decide for Adam was stepping on dangerous ground. It was Adam's right to choose.

When the barrister sat down, Fiona stared at her notes. Then she said, "Because this case is so unusual, I've decided that I would like to hear from Adam Henry himself. I want to find out how much he understands about his situation and what lies before him if I rule against the hospital. I shall explain that I am the one who will be making the decision in his best interests."

She went on to say that she would now travel with Mrs Greene to the hospital in Wandsworth, and would sit at Adam's bedside. When she returned to the court, she would give judgment.

CHAPTER FIVE

A cloth of beaten gold

It was about one of two things, Fiona decided as the taxi stopped in heavy traffic on Waterloo Bridge. She was either a woman on the edge of a nervous breakdown, making a serious mistake in her judgment. Or it was about a boy delivered from, or into, the beliefs of his religion by the court. It could not be both. At her side was Marina Greene, who was reading something on her phone. They had not spoken much. Fiona's phone was turned off, which was her only way of not checking texts and emails every five minutes. She had written but not sent a message: *You cannot do this!* But he *was* doing it, and she was a bloody fool. This emotional language was quite new to her. It was a mix of anger, loss and desire. She wanted him back; she never wanted to see him again. Guilt was also part of it, but what had she done? Lost herself to work, not given enough attention to her husband, let one case take all her time? But he had his own work and his different moods. She felt humiliated and didn't want anyone to know, and would behave as if everything was fine.

At last, they were on the Wandsworth Road, and she could see the huge Edith Cavell Hospital in front of them. She liked hospitals. When she was thirteen, she fell off her bicycle on the way to school and had to spend a very nice week in one. She remembered the kind nurses, and how clean everything was. The children's **ward** was full, so she had to be on an adult one. The other women there – some were seriously ill – were nice to her, and in the afternoons, her friends visited. Because she was young, she herself was well protected from disease and death. Before and after lunch, Fiona would sit alone with a notebook on her knees, planning her future – a pianist, a vet, a journalist, a singer. She thought of university and a nice husband, beautiful children, a sheep farm – the perfect life. Back then, she had not yet thought of the law. On the day she left, she went around the ward with her schoolbag over her shoulder saying goodbye to everyone while her mother watched.

From then on, she had always thought of hospitals as kind places, and now, as she stared out of the window at the hospital, she experienced a feeling of excitement.

She and Marina Greene entered the building and went through long corridors and up some stairs, until they found the lift. It took them to the ninth floor, and then another corridor took them to the **Intensive Care** ward. Two friendly nurses sat at the desk next to the entrance. They smiled and said hello to the two women, and then it was agreed that Fiona would wait outside while the social worker went in and explained things to Adam.

When Marina had gone through a door to the right, Fiona turned to the nurses and asked about their patient. "He's learning the violin," the first nurse said. "And driving us crazy!"

The other one laughed. "He's killing a cat in there."

"So what about this transfusion?" Fiona asked. They immediately stopped laughing.

Then, the first one said, "I pray for him every day. I say to Adam, 'God doesn't want you to do this, darling. He loves you anyway. God wants you to *live*.'"

"He's made his decision," said her friend, sadly. "You have to admire him, living for his faith."

"Dying you mean," said the first nurse. "That is a very confused boy in there."

Just then, Marina opened the door and raised a hand to Fiona before going back in.

Fiona said, "Well, thank you."

"You go in there and change his mind," said the first woman. "He's a lovely boy."

When Fiona later remembered stepping into Adam Henry's room, the picture in her mind was confused. There was a lot to see and understand. It was quite dark except for the light around the bed. Marina had just sat down in a corner with a magazine. The bed was surrounded by machines and tubes and bright screens that seemed to watch her silently, except that there was no silence because the boy was already talking to her. He was sitting up in the bed with pillows behind him. All around him were books, a laptop computer, a half-eaten orange, sweets, a notebook and many pages covered in writing. It was the ordinary teenage stuff – she recognized it from the many visits of her nieces and nephews.

He had a long narrow face. It was ghostly pale, but beautiful, with purple shadows under the eyes and lips which were purple, too. His eyes were huge and blue. He was very thin, and his arms hung like poles under the hospital clothes. He spoke quickly, **earnestly**, as he told her how strange it was, that he had always known that she would visit him, that he thought he could tell the future. They'd read a poem in school which said that future, past and present were all one, and this was what the Bible said, too. And, if God, poetry and science all said the same thing, it had to be true, didn't she think?

He fell back against the pillows, suddenly tired, and fought for his breaths. The fast bleeping sound from one of the machines told her how quickly his heart was beating – it was showing his excitement.

She slowly sat down in a chair. Then she leaned forward and said that she thought he was right. In court, if different people all said the same thing, then it was more likely to be true. "But not always," she added. "Sometimes people in a group can all share a **delusion** – they believe the same false idea. That certainly happens in courts of law."

"Like when?" Adam was still breathing fast and even these words were difficult to get out. He stared up at the ceiling while she thought of something to say.

"Some years ago, in this country, a number of children were taken into **care** by the **authorities**. Social workers believed that their parents had been doing terrible things to them. They said that the parents loved **Satan**, and what they were doing to their children was **satanic abuse**. Everyone hated the parents. Police, social workers, newspapers, even judges. But later, the evidence showed that the parents were innocent. It was a delusion. A dream. People felt stupid and guilty. And very slowly, the authorities returned the children to their homes."

Fiona talked as if she was in a dream. She felt happy and calm, even though she knew that Marina would be amazed by her words. What was the judge doing, talking to the boy about a subject like this, within minutes of meeting him? But what Marina thought did not really trouble her. She would do this her own way.

Adam lay still, taking in what she had said. At last, his breathing now under control, he turned his head on the pillow, and his eyes met hers. His look was dark and serious.

"The thing about Satan is that he's very good at putting an idea like satanic . . . what-did-you-say? Yes, abuse, into people's minds, and then they find out they're wrong, so everyone thinks he doesn't exist after all. Then he's free to do his worst."

"He's free to try and kill you with leukaemia?"

"Yes, that sort of thing."

"And you're going to let him?"

Adam pushed himself up, then touched his chin thoughtfully. "I plan to defeat him by obeying God. Have you come to change my mind? I think you have!" He was smiling widely now, his eyes bright and full of **innocence**. He kept changing how he behaved towards her. Now, he was the naughty child holding his knees, and he was excited again.

"I'll tell you why I'm here, Adam," Fiona said, patiently. "I want to be sure that you know what you're doing. Some people think that you're too young to be making a decision like this and you're just obeying your parents and the elders. And others think you're extremely clever and we should just let you do it."

"And how am I doing so far?"

He was playing a game with her, pulling her on to different ground where he could dance with her. He was trying to get

45

her to say something interesting again. It occurred to her then that he was simply bored and that by planning to take his own life he had made everything exciting. He was bringing lots of important adults to his bedside. If this was true, she liked him even more. Serious illness could not stop him from enjoying himself.

So how *was* he doing? "Quite well so far," she said. "You seem like someone who knows his own mind."

"Thank you," he said in a sweet voice.

"And if you know your own mind, you won't object to talking to me about your treatment. The doctor says that if he could transfuse you and add two drugs, you'd have a good chance of a complete and quick recovery. And without a transfusion you could die. You understand that?"

"Yes."

"And there's another possibility. Not death, Adam, but just some recovery. You could go blind, or your brain could be damaged. I'd just like to know that you've considered this carefully. That you may be ill and suffer for the rest of your life."

"I'd hate it, I'd hate it." He turned from her, clearly angry that she had so quickly cut into his good mood. "But I would have to accept it."

He was *so* thin. "Someone should take this boy home and feed him up," she thought.

One of the nurses came in to check the screens. She must have seen that Adam was upset because when she left she wiped the wetness from his eyes and said, "You listen carefully to what this lady has to say."

It lifted the mood in the room. Fiona didn't return to her next question. Instead, she nodded towards the papers on the bed. "I hear you've been writing poetry."

He seemed happy to be taken away from their last subject, and she noticed how quickly he could change.

"I've just finished something. I could read it to you if you like. It's really short."

He reached for a sheet of paper near his knee, and then he stopped to cough loudly. When he spoke again, his voice was weak.

"What do they call you in court?"

"Usually, it's My Lady, but you can call me Fiona."

"But I want to call you My Lady. It's wonderful. Please let me."

"All right. What about this poem?"

He leaned back against the pillows and stared at the sheet, trying to hear the poem through her ears. He was lovely but so weak and easy to hurt. He must be much loved at home, she decided. He looked at her quickly, breathed in, and began.

My happiness sank into the darkest hole
*When Satan took a **hammer** to my **soul**.*
He beat it long and slow
And I was low.
But Satan made a cloth of beaten gold.
That shone God's love upon all.
The way with gold light is paved
And I am saved.

She waited for more, but he put the page down and stared at the ceiling.

"I wrote it after one of the elders, Mr Crosby, told me that if the worst happened and I have to die, it would have a wonderful effect on everyone."

"He said that?" Fiona asked.

"It would fill our church with love."

"So Satan comes to destroy you with his hammer and, without intending to, he turns your soul into a sheet of gold that reflects God's love on everyone. And for this you're saved, and it doesn't matter so much that you're dead?"

"My Lady, you've understood it exactly," the boy almost shouted in his excitement. "Mr Crosby's going to try to get it published in the Jehovah's Witness magazine."

"That would be wonderful," she said. "You may have a future as a poet."

He saw what she was trying to do and smiled.

"What do your parents think of your poems?" she asked.

"My mum loves them, and my dad thinks they're OK, but he says they use the strength that I need to get better. But what does My Lady think? It's called 'The Hammer'."

He was so hungry for her to approve it that she paused. Then she said, "I think it's excellent. The shape of it. And those two short lines which balance everything. You're low, then you're saved. I like that. It's telling us that good things can come out of bad things. Isn't that right?"

"Yes."

"And I don't think you have to believe in God to understand or like this poem."

He thought for a moment and said, "I think you do."

She looked quickly down at her watch. She must soon return to the waiting court. He saw her do it.

"Don't go yet," he said. "Wait until they bring my supper."

"All right, Adam. Quickly, before I go. Show me your violin."

It was on the floor by the bed. She lifted it up and put it on his knees.

"It's only a school violin for beginners," he said, putting it under his chin. She hadn't planned for him to play, but she couldn't stop him. "I've been learning for four weeks, and I can play ten tunes. But this one is the hardest yet."

And then he began to play. She knew it well, this sad and lovely Irish song from the W. B. Yeats poem "Down by the Salley Gardens". She and Mark Berner had played it together many times. And suddenly, she began to sing with him.

In a field by the river my love and I did stand
And on my leaning shoulder she put her snow-white hand.
She told me take life easy, as the grass grows on the weirs;
But I was young and foolish, and am now full of tears.

As they finished, a man came into the room with Adam's dinner. Marina had already gone out with a strange look on her face.

Adam said, "Let's do it again."

Fiona shook her head as she took the violin from him and put it back under the bed.

"Stay just a bit longer. Please."

"Adam, I really have to go now."

"Then let me have your email."

"Mrs Justice Maye, Royal Courts of Justice, the Strand. That'll find me."

She lay her hand briefly on his cold wrist, then went towards the door without looking back.

CHAPTER SIX
A judgment

When Fiona entered the court, it was just after nine-fifteen. She waited for the room to become quiet and noticed the worried faces of the journalists. There might not be enough time left for the story to make the morning papers. In front of her sat the barristers and Marina Greene. Mr Henry was there but without his wife this time.

Fiona **summarized** the facts of the case and then said, "I have just returned from visiting Adam in hospital. I sat with him for an hour. He is clearly very ill. A doctor has told this court that by tomorrow, his situation will be very dangerous, which is why I am giving judgment late on a Tuesday evening." She thanked the barristers, Marina Greene and the hospital for helping her to come to a decision in a difficult case. She then summarized the history, the leukaemia and usual treatment which generally had good results. She said that Adam was having breathing problems. The defence had argued that Adam was three months short of his eighteenth birthday, was highly intelligent and his decisions should be considered as those of an adult. His faith was true and should be respected. "He is a very special child," Fiona said. "I might even say, as one of the nurses did this evening, that he is a lovely boy, and I'm sure his parents would agree. But I do not believe that he understands how ill he might become without the transfusion. In fact, he has a romantic idea about what it is to suffer. However . . ."

She let the word hang for a moment as she looked down at her notes.

"However, I am not guided by his understanding of his situation. I am guided instead by the decision of another judge – Mr Justice Ward – who also writes about a Jehovah's Witness case involving a teenager. '*The interests of the child are most important in my decision*.' I also have to think about Adam's wishes – that he does not want to have the transfusion. It is a right for all adults to say no to treatment, and Adam is prepared to die for his faith." She paused. "But I do not believe that Adam's mind and ideas are completely his own. He has only known life as a Jehovah's Witness, and so of course he will have the strong ideas of his faith. It will also not be good for his interests to suffer a terrible death. This court does not know if there is a heaven which, one day, Adam will discover or not. His interests are helped more by his love of poetry and his lively intelligence. He must be protected from his religion and from himself, so I rule against the wishes of Adam and his parents. It is lawful for the hospital to give Adam the treatments which they think are necessary."

It was almost eleven o'clock when Fiona left the Courts of Justice. She went to an all-night shop on Fleet Street to buy a ready meal. The night before, it would have been a dark and sad thing to do, but tonight she felt light and free – maybe because she hadn't eaten properly in two days. She bought a fish pie and some fruit, and gave her money to a young boy. She was singing "The Salley Gardens" to herself as she went along High Holborn. She would cook the pie while she got ready for bed, and eat it in front of the

TV while she watched the news. Then nothing could come between her and bed. Tomorrow's case was a divorce involving a famous guitarist and an almost-famous wife who wanted a large slice of his twenty-seven million.

She turned into Gray's Inn Square, loving the way that the sound of traffic died as she went through the gate and towards the buildings where many judges and barristers lived around a beautiful garden. They were interesting people who did interesting things − music, writing, fishing, even, and wine tasting. She loved it here and never wanted to leave.

She entered her building and noticed that the time-switch for the lights was on. She walked up to the second floor and turned into the corridor that led to her apartment. Then, she immediately understood why the light had been on. Her husband was there, just getting to his feet, a book in his hand. He looked both angry and humiliated. Behind him against the wall was his suitcase, which he had been using as a seat while he sat reading. Locked out. Working while waiting. And why not?

Her immediate thought − and it was a dark, selfish one − was that now she would have to share her fish pie with him. And then she thought she wouldn't. She'd rather not eat.

"I've been phoning you all evening," he said.

She unlocked the door and walked in without looking back. She went to the kitchen, put her stuff on the table and paused there. Her heart was beating much too hard. She heard his steps as he pulled in his suitcase along the corridor. Then, she went to her usual place on the chaise longue and began reading through some papers.

Jack entered and went to get himself a drink, then offered her one, which she refused. He wore jeans and a white shirt, and he hadn't shaved. He crossed the room to his chair and sat down heavily. His chair, her chair, married life again.

Then, he said, "Look, Fiona, I love you."

After several seconds she said, "I'd rather you slept in the other room."

He nodded slowly but did not get up.

They both knew all the things that were not being said. That she had allowed him into the flat meant that he could sleep here. He had not told her yet whether the statistician had ordered him to go or he had changed his mind. He had not spoken about the change of locks. What they needed now was a huge argument with lots of accusations. There would be several chapters to it, and it would take place over a long period of time. His guilt would come in angry complaining words. She would tell him how humiliated he had made her feel. It might be months before she would allow him into her bed again, with the ghost of the other woman moving around them. But she knew that they would find a way of getting back, more or less, to what they once had.

The thought of the huge effort involved tired her further. Yet she had to do it. Like a contract she had signed. She realized that she would like a drink after all, but that might have looked too much like she wanted to celebrate. Most of all, she could not bear to hear again that he loved her. She wanted to be in bed alone. What was to stop her? She stood and picked up her papers, and it was then that he started to speak.

He talked for a long time. He said he was sorry, he tried to explain his actions, he talked earnestly about his age and his faithfulness to her before Melanie. He said how, as soon as he had arrived at Melanie's place, he realized his mistake. She was a stranger, he didn't understand her. And when they went into her bedroom . . .

Fiona put up a hand. She didn't want to hear about the bedroom. He paused, considered and continued. He was a bloody fool, he realized, to be driven by sexual need, and he should have come back the night that he left, but he was embarrassed and felt he had to continue. "Everything we have," he said, "everything we've made together, this love that –"

"I've had a long day," Fiona said, and crossed the room.

She stopped by the kitchen to take an apple and a banana from her shopping on the table. Having them in her hand brought back into her mind her happy walk home from work. She had felt the beginnings of something becoming easier. It was hard to bring that back now. She pushed open the door and saw his suitcase standing on its wheels by the bed. Then it came to her what she felt about Jack's return. So simple. She was disappointed that he had not stayed away. Just a little longer.

CHAPTER SEVEN

A quiet conflict

It seemed to Fiona that in the late summer of 2012, everyone was suffering from marriage break-ups in Great Britain. Loving promises were broken. Partners who had once been trusted now hid behind their lawyers, not caring about the costs. Documents were changed, shared objects were fought over, trust was replaced by "arrangement", and love revealed itself as a delusion.

And the confused children? They were stuck between warring mothers and fathers, pushed between their separate houses, toys, coats and pencils sometimes forgotten or left behind, with these facts occasionally reported to the lawyers. One parent was often accused of abuse, usually they were accused by mothers, sometimes by fathers. Sometimes, the children spent half the time with one parent and half with the other. Sometimes, they could only see their fathers once or twice a month, or maybe never, as some men just disappeared into new marriages to make new children.

And the money? Greedy husbands challenged greedy wives, taking what they could from the end of the war before both armies went their own ways. Men sent their money to foreign bank accounts, women wanted an easy life in which they would never have to work again. Mothers stopping their children from seeing their fathers, fathers not supporting their children. Husbands hitting wives, wives lying and angry, drinking or taking drugs. The work of the Family Division went on.

And there Fiona was, in **conflict** herself. Sometimes, she thought she would like to send them all to prison, these people who put their needs above the interests of their children. The ones who wanted a younger wife, a richer or less boring husband, a different house, fresh sex, fresh love, a new world, a nice new start before it was too late. It was all about chasing pleasure. Of course she was not serious when she thought this, and she knew that her anger was because she had no children herself, and because of Jack. As part of these secret thoughts, he would have been sent to prison for spoiling their marriage in order to try something new. And why not?

For life at home in Gray's Inn since his return was difficult. There had been arguments, and she had shown some angry feelings. He said sorry again and again, but also complained in his defence that she was distant from him, that she was cold. He even said one night that she was "no fun" and "did not know how to play" any more. This made her more angry than anything since she knew that it might be true.

At least he was no longer saying that he loved her. Their most recent argument, ten days ago, repeated all the accusations they had made before, and they then stopped, tired of each other and themselves. Since then, nothing. They went about their days, their separate working lives in different parts of the city, and when in the apartment, moved softly and quietly around each other. They did not have meals together; they worked in separate rooms and refused any invitations to dinner or parties. She had given him a new key, that was all.

She understood from the things that he had said that he had not found ecstasy in the statistician's bed, but that didn't make her feel better. Might he look for it somewhere else? Maybe he was already looking for it. She remembered her promise to leave him if he slept with Melanie, but she did not have the time or energy to organize the break-up of her marriage. And she was still unsure, she did not trust her mood at the moment. If he had given her more time after he left, she would have reached a clear decision and worked to end the marriage or try to save it. So she threw herself into her work in the usual way and tried to survive one day at a time.

When one of his nieces left her children with them for the weekend, twin girls aged eight, things were easier because they could concentrate on something outside of themselves. She would read them stories, and as she was speaking, a wave of love for them rose in her throat. She was feeling old and foolish. It troubled her to be reminded how good Jack was with children as she watched him play games with them in the garden, and act out the stories he read them with different loud voices.

But on Sunday evening, after the twins had left, the rooms became small again and the air full of quiet conflict. Then Jack went out without explanation. To meet someone, she wondered, as she tidied up the **spare** room, putting toys back in the cupboard with that feeling of sadness and emptiness that can come when children suddenly leave. That feeling stayed with her into Monday morning and only began to fade when she sat at her desk to prepare for her first case of the week.

At some point Nigel Pauling must have brought in the post, for the pile was suddenly there at her elbow. She noticed a small blue envelope resting on the top. She nearly called back her clerk to open it for her as she saw the strange, large handwriting and the stamp not quite in the right place. She expected it to be more badly written abuse from someone she'd ruled against. But then she saw the postmark and, suddenly suspecting who it was from, opened it quickly and saw that she was right. She had been expecting it for weeks. She had spoken to Marina Greene and knew that Adam was doing well, catching up on school work at home and was expected to return to his classroom soon.

My Lady!

  This is my seventh, and I think it's going to be the one that I post.

The first few words of the next paragraph had been drawn through with a line of pen.

  *It will be the simplest and the shortest. I only want to describe to you one event. I realize now how important it is. It's changed everything. I'm glad I waited because I wouldn't want you to see the other letters I wrote. Too embarrassing! But not as terrible as the names I called you when the nurse told me your decision. I was sure you'd seen things my way. In fact, I know exactly what you told me, that it was obvious that I knew my own mind, and I remember thanking you. I was still shouting when that awful doctor Rodney Carter came in with the others. They thought that they were going to have to hold me down, but I was too weak for that. Although I was so angry, I knew what you wanted me to do. So I held out my arm and they started. The thought of someone's blood going into me was so horrible that I was **sick** across the bed.*

But that isn't what I wanted to tell you. It's this. My mum couldn't bear to watch, so she was sitting outside my room, and I could hear her crying, and I felt really sad. I was sick again, and then I fainted. When I woke up, my parents were both there by my bed, and they were crying. Then I felt even sadder, because we had all disobeyed God. But this is the important thing. It took me a while to realize that they were both crying for JOY!

They were so happy, hugging me and each other and thanking God, and crying at the same time. I felt too strange, and I didn't work it out for a few days. I didn't think about it. But then it came to me. That thing people say, "Have your cake and eat it." I never understood that saying before, but now I do. Your cake is still in your hand even though you've eaten it. My parents obeyed the elders and did everything that was right – and at the same time they can still have me alive. Transfused, but we didn't choose it! Blame the judge, blame the godless law, blame the world. Thank God! We still have our son even though we said he must die. Our son, the cake!

I don't know what to think about this. Has it all been a lie? It was a turning point for me. When they brought me home, I moved the Bible out of my room and put it in the hall face down on a chair, and I told my parents that I did not believe in the faith any more, and they can throw me out of the community if they like. We've had some terrible arguments. Mr Crosby has visited, but I won't listen to him. I've been writing to you because I really need to hear your calm voice and have your clear mind discuss this with me. I feel you've brought me close to something else, something really beautiful and deep, but I don't know what it is. You never told me what you believed in, but I loved it when you came and sat with me and we did "The Salley Gardens". I still look at that poem every day. I love being "young and foolish", and if it wasn't for you, I'd be neither. I'd be dead! I wrote you lots of stupid letters, and I think about you all the time and really want to see you and talk again. I daydream about us, impossible, wonderful dreams, like we go on a journey together round the world in a ship, and we walk up and down on it talking all day.

My Lady, will you please write to me, just a few words to say that you've read this letter and you don't hate me for writing it.

Yours,

Adam Henry

PS I forgot to say that I'm getting stronger all the time.

She didn't post the note that took her almost an hour that evening to write. In her fourth and final draft, she thought that she sounded friendly enough. She was glad to learn that he was home and feeling better, pleased that he had good memories of her visit. She told him to be loving towards his parents and that it was normal to question things when you were a teenager. She finished by saying, although it was not true, that she had smiled at the idea of a boat trip around the world. She wrote that, when she'd been young, she'd had dreams of escape just like his own. That wasn't true either because she'd been too hungry, even at sixteen, to do well at school to think about running away. Teenage visits to her cousins in Newcastle had been her only adventures.

But, when she looked at her short letter a day later, she did not find it friendly but cold and distant. She read his again and loved its earnest, warm words. No, better to send nothing than to make him feel bad. If she changed her mind, she could write later.

CHAPTER EIGHT

On circuit

The time was approaching when Fiona would be on circuit, visiting cities in the north of England with another judge to hear cases, so that the families involved did not have to travel the long distance to London. She would stay in special **lodgings** – huge beautiful town houses where wines of great quality were kept and food was made for her by excellent cooks. The bedrooms were grander than her own at home and the beds wider. In previous times, as a happily married woman, she had enjoyed escaping to the guilty pleasure of such an unshared accommodation. Now, she was desperate to leave the silent conflict at home, and her first stop was her favourite English city.

One morning in early September, a week before she began her journey, she received a second letter. No address, only her name. This time she was more worried, even before she opened it, for the blue envelope had been pushed under their apartment door. It was easy enough for Adam Henry to wait outside the Courts of Justice and follow her home at a distance.

Jack had already left for work. She sat down at the breakfast table.

My Lady,

I don't even know what I wrote because I didn't keep a copy, but it's OK that you didn't reply. I still need to talk to you. Here's my news. Big arguments with my parents, great to be back at *school, feeling better, feeling happy and then sad and then happy again. Sometimes, the idea of having a stranger's blood inside me makes me **sick**. Sometimes, I keep thinking that transfusion is wrong, but I don't care any more. I've got so many questions for you, but I'm not sure that you remember me. You must have had many cases since me. I feel jealous! I wanted to come and talk to you in the street, but I couldn't do it because I'm not brave. I thought you might not recognize me. You haven't got to reply to this one either – which means I wish you would. Please don't worry, I'm not going to chase you around all the time and become obsessed or anything like that. I just feel the top of my head has exploded. All kinds of things are coming out!*

Yours sincerely,

Adam Henry

Immediately, she emailed Marina Greene to ask if she could find time to visit the boy and report back. By the end of the day, she had a reply. Marina had met Adam that afternoon at his school. He had gained weight, there was colour in his cheeks. He was doing extra work for his exams before Christmas. He was full of joy and fun. There was some trouble at home, mostly because of religious differences, but she thought that there was nothing unusual about that. Separately, his teachers told her that Adam had done well in his time after hospital to catch up with his schoolwork. Feeling better, Fiona decided against writing to him.

———

A week later, on the morning that she was leaving for the north-east of England, a tiny thing happened between her and Jack which told her a lot. Fiona thought about it as the train pulled out of London. She had come into the kitchen to find Jack using the coffee machine. He liked his coffee very strong, as did she. Her suitcase was in the hall, and she was putting the last of her papers together. He poured some milk into his coffee, turned and raised the cup a little, and their eyes met quickly. Then, he put it down on the table, pushing it towards her. This might not have meant much normally, because they were always very polite as they silently moved around each other, as if they were competing for a prize. But there are ways of putting down a cup on a table, and there are ways of accepting it. She took it, and lifting it to her mouth, swallowed a little. And then she remained there. A few seconds passed, and this seemed as far as they were prepared to go. It was as if the moment contained too much for them and to try more would have damaged them. He turned to make another cup for himself, and she slowly moved towards the bedroom to get a scarf.

By the early afternoon, she was in Newcastle and being driven to the law courts on the riverside. Nigel Pauling was waiting for her by the judge's entrance, and he led her to her room. Then they went through the cases listed for the days ahead. It was not until four that she was free to leave. There was rain in the air as she told her driver to wait while she went for a walk by the river. She liked this city with its huge metal bridge. A city which had been built on industry, but was now full of fashionable cafés and bars. She had come here several times as a teenager, when her mother was ill, to stay with her cousins. Their house was busy and a bit crazy, a big change from the clean, organized calm of her mother's house. Her Uncle Fred, a dentist, was the wealthiest man she had ever known. Aunt Simone taught French at a school. Her cousins were a bit wild and liked to take her out in the evenings on adventures which included drinking beer and wine and meeting musicians with long hair. Her parents would have been very worried to know what she was doing there. She went to clubs and had taken her first lover, Keith, who sang in a band. Along with her cousins, she worked as a roadie – carrying drums and guitars around for the band. If she had been able to stay longer, she might have married Keith and become a singer. But her Uncle Fred moved south when she was eighteen, and her relationship with Keith ended in tears and some love poems which she didn't send.

This wild period in her life, which was full of excitement and risk, was something that she would never experience again, and she always thought of it when she thought of Newcastle. She could never have lived like that in London, where she was following her career in the law. She had been to the north-east many times since, four on circuit, and she was always excited to step off the train at Newcastle Central Station. She loved to stand there and smell the fresher air, see the city's beautiful buildings, and remember seeing her uncle and cousins waiting there for her. It always made her think of the possibility of another life unlived, even as her sixtieth birthday approached.

———

A large car took her through a park to her lodgings – Leadman Hall was a beautiful, very grand old white building with twelve bedrooms. Nine servants worked there, looking after the two

High Court judges who would be there on circuit. Pauling was waiting with the **butler** by the main door. They led her to her room on the first floor. It was at the front of the house, with three tall windows which looked out over the trees and lake. Her bathroom was along a corridor.

The storm arrived as she returned from her bath. She stood at the centre window with a towel around her and watched the trees bend in the rain and wind. Then, she turned on the lights and began to dress. She was already ten minutes late for drinks in the **drawing room**.

Four men wearing dark suits and holding glasses stopped talking and rose from their armchairs as she entered. A waiter in a stiff white jacket mixed her drink while her colleague, Caradoc Ball, who was doing the criminal list, introduced her to the others. They were all connected to Ball in some way. She had not invited guests for the first evening. They talked about the violent weather, and all the while she was wondering why the waiter was taking so long. Finally, he brought her drink and a minute later the butler appeared and told the group that dinner was ready.

The four men finished their drinks and followed Fiona from the drawing room through to the dining room. The table, which could have seated thirty guests, had five lonely dining places made ready at its far end. The dining room was at the north of the house where the wind blew and the windows shook. The air was cold and damp. The butler explained that the fire could not be lit, but he could bring a small heater for them.

The five of them chatted while white wine was poured into their glasses and cold fish and toast was put before them. One of the men, Charlie, who was a professor who worked for the government, asked about Fiona's work, and she told him about the case that she would hear the next day. A local **authority** wanted to take two children – a boy of two and a girl of four – into care. The mother drank too much and took drugs. She was no longer able to look after herself or her children. The father, after not being around for most of the children's lives, had now appeared with his new girlfriend and decided that they could do the caring. A social worker would give evidence in court tomorrow about his ability to be a parent. The mother's parents loved the children and wanted to have them, but had no rights. There had been terrible arguments between the three groups.

There were, she said, many more cases like it listed for the week. Charlie put his hand to his head and closed his eyes. If he had to make a decision like that, he said, he'd be up all night thinking about it.

Caradoc Ball, who was an old school friend of Charlie's, said, "I hope you realize just how well-known a judge you are talking to. I'm sure you all remember the conjoined twins case."

Everyone did, and as the plates were cleared they were asking her questions about that famous case, when there came the sound of loud voices in the hall outside. Then, Pauling and the butler came in and approached her. Pauling, after apologizing to the four men, leaned over and whispered in her ear.

"My Lady, I'm sorry, but there's a problem which needs your immediate attention."

She nodded and stood up. "Excuse me, gentlemen."

They all rose and she walked with the two men across the

room. When she was outside, she said to the butler, "We're still waiting for that heater."

"I'll fetch it now."

There was something sharp in the way he said it, and she turned to look at her clerk with surprise. But Pauling simply said, "It's this way."

She followed him across the hallway and into a huge dark library.

Pauling said, "It's that Jehovah's Witness boy, Adam Henry. Do you remember, from the transfusion case? He seems to have followed you here. He's been walking through the rain and is wet-through. They wanted to send him away, but I thought you should know first."

"Where is he now?" asked Fiona.

"He's in the kitchen."

"Better bring him in then."

CHAPTER NINE
The visitor

As soon as Pauling had left, Fiona got up and walked slowly around the room, feeling her heartbeat increasing. If she'd answered Adam Henry's letters, she wouldn't be facing this now. But facing what, exactly? Unnecessary contact with a case that was closed? And more than that. But there was no time to consider. She heard footsteps approaching.

The door swung open, and Pauling brought in the boy. She had never seen him out of bed and was surprised by how tall he was. He wore his school clothes: grey trousers and sweater, white shirt, a thin jacket now all wet, and his hair was damp and untidy. A small bag hung from his shoulder.

The boy took a couple of steps and stopped close to where she stood and said, "I'm truly sorry."

In those first moments, it was easier to hide her confusion behind worry for him. "You look frozen," she said. "We'd better bring that heater in here."

"I'll bring it myself," Pauling said, and left.

"Well," she said after a silence. "How did you find me here?"

"I followed you in a taxi to King's Cross and got on your train. I didn't know where you'd get off, so I had to buy a ticket to Edinburgh. At Newcastle, I followed you out through the station entrance and saw you get into a big car, so I asked people where the law courts were. When I got there, I saw your car."

She watched him as he spoke, noticing the changes in him.

No longer thin, but still slim. Stronger in his shoulders and arms. Same long, beautiful face. He seemed alive, passionate and hungry for life.

"I waited a really long time," he went on. "Then you came out, and I followed you through the town until you got back in the car. I looked for judges' lodgings on my phone and this place came up. So I got a taxi here, climbed over the wall and waited outside wondering what to do. Then someone saw me."

Pauling, looking red-faced and unhappy, came back in with the heater and turned it on. He put his hands on the young man's shoulders and moved him in front of the warm air. Before he left, he said to Fiona, "I'll be right outside."

When they were alone, she said, "Shouldn't I think there's something scary about you following me home and then here?"

"Oh no!" he cried. "Please don't think that. It's not like that." He looked around quickly. "Look, you saved my life. And it's not only that. My dad tried to keep it from me, but I read your judgment. You said you wanted to protect me from my religion. Well you have. I'm saved!"

He laughed at his own joke, and she said, "I didn't save you so that you could follow me across the whole of the country."

The fan heater made a strange sound and went bright red, then it slowly went back to normal. She suddenly felt angry with the whole place. These lodgings were cold and damp. Everything was old and needed work. How had she not noticed before?

"Do your parents know where you are?" she asked.

"I'm eighteen. I can be where I like."

71

"I don't care how old you are. They'll be worried."

He put his bag down on the floor. "Look, My Lady –"

"Enough of that. It's Fiona." As long as she could keep him in his place she felt better. "Now what about your parents?"

"Yesterday I had a huge argument with my dad. We've had a few since I came out of hospital, but this one was really big. We were both shouting, and I told him everything I thought about his stupid religion. In the end I walked out. I went up to my room, packed my bag, got all the money I had and said goodbye to my mum. Then I left."

"You must phone her now."

"No need. I texted her last night from where I was staying."

"Text her again."

He looked at her, both surprised and disappointed.

"Tell her you're safe and happy in Newcastle and you'll write again tomorrow. Then we'll talk."

She stood and watched while he quickly sent a text. In seconds, the phone was back in his pocket.

"There," he said, and looked at her as if she was the one who had questions to answer.

She crossed her arms. "Adam, why are you here?"

He looked away and paused. He was not going to tell her, or not directly.

"Look," he said. "I'm not the same person. When you came to see me, I was ready to die. It's amazing that people like you could waste your time on me. I was such an idiot."

She pointed to two chairs by an old wooden table, and they sat facing each other across it. The too-bright ceiling light shone down on them, lighting his cheekbones and lips. It really was a beautiful face.

"I didn't think that you were an idiot."

"But I was. Whenever the doctors and nurses tried to make me change my mind, I just felt like a hero telling them to leave me alone. I was pure and good. I liked it that my parents and elders were proud of me. At night, when no one was there, I imagined myself making a video on my phone. I wanted it to be played on the television news after I died and for everyone to be proud of me and love me. I was *such* an idiot."

"And where was God in all this?"

"Behind everything. These were his instructions I was obeying. It was mostly about the wonderful adventure I was on. I would die beautifully and be loved by everyone. This girl I know at school stopped eating three years ago, when she was fifteen. She dreamed of becoming so thin that she died, like a dry leaf in the wind. She wanted everyone to feel sorry for her and blame themselves afterwards for not understanding her. It's the same sort of thing with me."

Fiona thought about him in that hospital bed. It wasn't his illness that came back to her, it was his excitement and innocence.

"So this wasn't so much about your religion then," she said. "More about your feelings."

"My feelings came out of my religion. I was doing what God wanted, and you and everyone who didn't share my faith were just wrong. How could I have got myself into such a mess without being a Jehovah's Witness?"

"It sounds like your school friend managed it."

"Yes, well, I wanted the same thing as her. You know, wanting to suffer, loving the pain and thinking that everyone's watching and caring and the whole world is about you. And your weight!"

She couldn't stop herself from laughing. He smiled at his success at amusing her.

They heard voices and footsteps in the hallway as the guests left the dining room and crossed to the sitting room for coffee. The boy looked worried, and they sat together in silence waiting for the sounds to fade. Adam looked down at his hands.

"Adam, I'm asking you again. Why are you here?"

"To thank you."

"There are easier ways."

He breathed out heavily and put his hands in his pockets. For a moment, she thought that he was getting ready to leave.

"Your visit was one of the best things that ever happened to me," he said, passionately. Then, quickly, "My parents' religion was a poison, and you removed it from inside me."

"I don't remember talking about your parents' faith."

"You didn't. You were calm, you listened, you asked questions, and then you said a few things. It's this thing you have, a way of thinking and talking. If you don't know what I mean, go and listen to the elders. And when we did our song . . ."

She said, quickly, "Are you still playing the violin?"

He nodded.

"And the poetry?"

"Yes, lots. But I hate the stuff I was writing before."

"Well, you're good. I know you'll write something wonderful."

She saw the sadness in his eyes. She was stepping back, being the kind aunt. She took a couple of steps back through the conversation, wondering why she was so worried about disappointing him.

"And what is this *thing* I'm supposed to have?" she said.

"When I saw my parents crying like that, really crying, and laughing with joy, everything became obvious to me. Of course they didn't want me to die. They love me. Why didn't they say that instead of always talking about the faith? That's when I saw the situation as an ordinary human. Ordinary and good. It was like an adult had come into a room full of kids and said, 'Come on, stop all this nonsense. It's tea time.' You were the adult. You knew, but you didn't say. '*All of love and life that lie ahead of him —*' that's what you wrote in your judgment. Everything changed after 'The Salley Gardens'. Fiona, I can almost get through this piece of music by Bach without making a mistake. I'm going to be in a play, and thanks to you, I'm full of Yeats."

"Yes," she said, quietly. Then, as he leaned forward on his elbows, his face hungry and excited, she got up. "Wait here."

She paused for a moment, then went outside and spoke to Pauling quietly. When she returned, she said, "So what are you going to do now? Where are you going to go?"

He wasn't happy about the question. "I've got an aunt in Birmingham. My mother's sister. She'll have me for a week or two."

"She's expecting you?"

"Yes. I mean, well, I think she is . . ."

She was about to make him send another text, when he reached his hand across the table, and just as quickly, she pulled hers back and put it on her knees.

He put his face in his hands and couldn't bear to look at her as he spoke. "This is my question. When you hear it, you'll think it's so stupid. But please don't just reject it. Please say you'll think about it."

"Well?"

"I want to come and live with you."

She waited for more. She could never have guessed that he would ask this, but now it seemed obvious.

He had thought about it hard. "I could do jobs for you, housework and shopping. And you could give me lists of books to read, you know, everything you think I should know about."

He had followed her through the country, through the streets, walked through a storm, to ask her. It was one step further on from his dream of walking and talking all day on that ship. Crazy, but innocent.

After a long silence, she said, "You know that isn't possible."

"I wouldn't get in the way, I mean, with you and your husband." Finally, he looked up at her. "When I've finished my exams, I could get a job and pay you some rent."

She thought about the spare room and its two beds, the toys in the cupboard, so many of them that sometimes the door would not close. At last, without turning, she said, "We only have one spare room and lots of nephews and nieces."

"You mean that's your *only* objection?"

There was a knock on the door, and Pauling came in. "It will be here in two minutes, My Lady," he said, and left again.

She rose to her feet and leaned down to pick up Adam's bag from the floor.

"My clerk will go with you in a taxi, first to the station to buy you a ticket to Birmingham tomorrow, and then to a hotel close by."

After a pause, he got slowly to his feet and took the bag from her. Despite his height, he looked like a small child in shock.

"Is that it then?" he said.

"I'd like you to promise me that you'll contact your mother again before you get on the train. Tell her where you'll be."

He didn't reply. He followed her to the door, and they went out into the hall. There was no one there. Caradoc Ball and his guests were in the sitting room, behind closed doors. The front door was open, and the butler was talking to the driver who had loud music coming from his taxi. Pauling was crossing the hall towards the driver, probably worried that the butler would create a problem.

The boy started to say, "We haven't even –" but she raised a hand to stop him.

"You must go."

Lightly, she took the edge of his thin jacket between her fingers and pulled him towards her. Her plan was to kiss him on the cheek, but as she reached up and he bent low, he turned his head and their lips met. She could have pulled back, she could have stepped away from him, but she didn't. She stayed there for a few moments, the feeling of his skin on hers taking away any choice. It was more than a kiss that a mother might give her adult son. Over in two seconds, perhaps three. Time enough to feel the softness of his lips, of all the life and all the years that lay between her and him. They pulled slowly apart and may have come back

77

together again, but there were footsteps approaching on the steps outside. She let go of his jacket and said again, "You must go."

He followed her out into the fresh night air. The driver got out and opened the door for him while she gave some money to Pauling. She had intended to give it to Adam, but suddenly changed her mind. Adam got into the taxi and stared straight ahead. The music had been turned off.

Already regretting what she had started, Fiona moved around the car to look at him, but he turned his head away. Pauling got in the front next to the driver while the butler closed Adam's door.

Wrapping her arms tightly around herself, Fiona hurried up the stone steps as the taxi drove off.

CHAPTER TEN

The sweetest kiss

She moved on from Newcastle after a week, her judgments made. In the case that she had described to Charlie at dinner, she gave the children to the grandparents and allowed weekly visits from the mother and father separately. In the late afternoon of Friday, she said goodbye to her colleagues at the court. On Saturday morning, Pauling drove them west to the city of Carlisle.

As they slowed in heavy traffic, Fiona's phone lay in her hand, and she was thinking, as she had done often through the week, of the kiss. How stupid of her not to have stopped it. It was professional and social madness. She tried to act like it was just something quick and innocent, but each time it grew in her mind until she no longer knew what it was or what had happened. Caradoc Ball could have stepped into the hall at any moment. Or one of his guests might have seen her. Pauling could have turned back from his conversation with the driver and surprised her. Then the formal, polite distance between them which made her work possible would have been destroyed.

She did not usually do wild things, and she did not understand why she had behaved like that. She realized that there was more to her feelings than just professional worries, but at the moment this was what filled her mind. It was hard to believe that no one had seen them, that she had escaped without anyone knowing about her crime. Maybe someone *had* seen her and miles away in

London they were discussing it now. She imagined the voice on the phone of an embarrassed colleague, "Ah, Fiona, look, I'm sorry, but I should warn you that something's happened."

She decided to call her husband, knowing that she was running from a kiss to the safety of her marriage. She made the call from habit, without thinking about how things were between her and Jack. When she heard his careful "hello" echo slightly, she knew he was in the kitchen. She could hear the radio playing.

He asked her if she was all right and she replied "fine". It surprised her how normal she sounded. She reminded him of her return date at the end of the month and suggested that, on the evening she came home, they should go out for a meal together. They usually did this when she returned from circuit. He said in a surprised voice that he thought it was a good idea. He asked her again if she was all right, and she repeated that she was fine.

It had worked. She was lifted from her worries into the firmness of an arrangement, a date. It was good to have phoned and moved things on from that strange breakfast moment. The world was not how she had worriedly dreamed it. An hour later, they were driving into Carlisle, and she was concentrating on court papers.

And so two weeks later, her circuit complete, she faced her husband in a quiet corner of a restaurant near their apartment. A bottle of wine stood between them, which they were drinking slowly. They did not talk about their relationship – the subject which might have destroyed them. He spoke to her awkwardly, like she was some kind of bomb which might explode. She asked him about his work.

Later, when they had covered the safe subjects, there came a worrying silence. She kept thinking about what he had done, leaving her to be with Melanie. And she knew that he felt she was making too much of it.

The end of the war between them was not quick. They began to eat meals together again, to go to supper together with friends. But he still slept in the spare room, and when a nineteen-year-old nephew came to stay, he slept on the sofa.

Late October came. The clocks went back, and the darkness closed in. Not much changed between her and Jack, but she was too busy and too tired to start the big conversations that might move them to a new stage. In the evenings, if she had the energy, she practised alone at the piano to prepare for a Christmas concert with Mark Berner at the Royal Courts of Justice's Great Hall. Jack was busy, too, doing the work of a sick colleague at the university.

At the end of October, as Fiona looked through her morning post at the courts, she found another blue envelope. Pauling was in the room at the time. When he had left, she opened it. Adam had sent her an unfinished poem. There was no letter with it.

THE SONG OF ADAM HENRY
I took my wooden cross and laid it by the stream
I was young and foolish and worried by a dream
That punishment was stupid, the type of thing for fools

But I'd been told on Sundays to live life by the rules.
The cross cut into my shoulder, it was heavy as lead
My life was narrow and godly, and I was almost dead
The stream was happy and dancing, and sunlight danced around
But I must keep on walking, with eyes fixed to the ground.
Then a fish jumped out of the water, with rainbows on its scales
The water danced around it and hung in silver tails
"Throw your cross into the water, if you're wanting to be free!"
So I drowned my cross in the water, in the shade of the Judas tree.
I kneeled by the river and felt full of bliss
While she leaned on my shoulder and gave the sweetest kiss
Then she jumped into its icy bottom, where she'll never more be found.
And I was full of tears until I heard the music sound.
And God stood on the water, and He said this to me
"That fish was the voice of Satan, and you must pay the fine.
*Her kiss was the kiss of **Judas**, her kiss sold my name.*
May he

May he what? The last words were lost to lines of pen which went around and around. Words taken out, put back, taken out. She read the poem again then sat back with her eyes closed. She didn't like it that he was angry with her, thinking she was Satan. In her head, she started writing a letter to him that she knew she would never send. *I had to send you away. It was in your own interests. You have your own young life to lead. Even if we had the room, you could not live with us. This is simply not possible for a judge. Adam, I'm not Judas. An old lady, perhaps . . .*

Her "sweetest kiss" had been crazy, and she had not escaped

her crime, not in his eyes. It was kinder not to reply to him. He would write straight back to her if she did. He would be at her door, and she'd have to make him go away again. She put the poem back in the envelope and later put it in her bedside table. He would soon move on and do brilliantly in his exams, then go to a good university. He would forget her.

CHAPTER ELEVEN
The last song

In December, on the day of the concert with Mark Berner, she was home from court by six and hurrying to shower and change her clothes. She heard Jack in the kitchen and called hello to him as she passed on her way to her bedroom. Forty minutes later, she appeared in the hall in a black dress and high shoes. Around her neck she wore a silver necklace. Jack had put on a record. It was jazz music – Keith Jarrett's *Facing You*. She paused to listen to it. It was a long time since she had heard it, remembering now how the piano started gently and then gradually grew stronger until it filled the whole room.

She knew that Jack was sending her a message with this music. They had listened to it at the beginning of their relationship, those first few days and weeks after her university exams when he had invited her to spend first one, then many nights in the room which looked out over the Thames. In that room, she had understood that ecstasy was possible and had screamed with joy. When they had finished making love, she had told him that she did not have enough strength left in her bones to ever do it again. But she did, many times. She was young.

It was around that time that Jack started trying to get her to play jazz on the piano. He bought her sheet music to learn from, but she did not find it easy. It allowed for too much freedom, too much playing by *feeling*. Her fingers needed to follow the rules, the notes as they were written. That was why she was studying law, she told her lover.

She gave up, but she did learn to enjoy listening, and it was Jarrett she loved above all others.

She went along the hall and paused again at the entrance to the sitting room. Jack had lit candles around the room and was standing by the fire with a bottle of expensive wine in his hand. There was a plate of biscuits, fruit and cheese on the low table in front of him. She moved towards him as he poured a glass of wine and gave it to her, then poured another for himself. They raised and touched their glasses.

"We haven't got much time."

She thought that he meant that they should be leaving to walk to the Great Hall. It was crazy to be drinking before a concert, but she didn't care. She swallowed another mouthful and then followed him to the table. He offered her the plate, and she took some cheese.

"Who knows how much," he said. "Not many years. Either we start living again, really living, or we give up and are unhappy for the rest of our lives."

This was something he had always believed. Life is short, and we must try to enjoy every moment.

She lifted the glass. "To living again."

She saw the sudden happiness in his face. "That dress is amazing," he said. "You look beautiful."

"Thank you."

They stared at each other and then went towards each

other and kissed. They kissed again. If they didn't have the concert to go to, she wondered how this might end, but her sheet music was behind her on the chaise longue. They slowly moved apart then lifted their glasses one more time and drank.

She held his arm as they walked together to the Great Hall. A crowd of around a hundred and fifty people waited for them, standing around the room with glasses of wine. They were mostly judges, lawyers and barristers. For more than thirty years, she had worked with or against them. She moved around, talking to different groups, quickly losing Jack. Friends came up to hug her and wish her luck. It had been a great idea of the organizers to have a party before the concert.

A waiter came by with a tray, and she took a third glass of wine. Then Mark Berner appeared and waved a finger to warn her that she shouldn't be drinking. He was right, of course. She raised her glass to him and took a mouthful anyway, then put down the glass. She continued speaking to different groups around the hall until, finally, Mark approached her, and she followed him to the steps which led to the stage. As she did, she felt a hand on her arm. It was Sherwood Runcie, a barrister from the Moroccan case who wanted to tell her about something interesting which was connected to her. It had been kept out of the newspapers. She leaned towards him to catch his words, and at the same time, saw Mark look back at her impatiently. She thanked Runcie and went to join Mark at the bottom of the steps. They paused there to wait for the audience to take their seats.

"Are you all right?" Mark said as they waited.

"I'm fine. Why?"

"You look pale."

A loud cheer followed as they slowly climbed the steps. She sat down at the piano, and he stood next to it. This was followed by silence. Then Mark nodded to her. Immediately, the gentle notes rose from under her fingers. They moved through Berlioz's "Villanelle" and "Lament". Very quickly, the two of them relaxed together as they performed. She loved the falling words, *Ah! Sans amour s'en aller sur la mer!* This was followed by Mahler, which Mark sang in English rather than German. Her own playing looked after itself, she only needed to be there. The couple knew that they were holding their audience, and their playing grew better and better. The music took Fiona away from herself, but as she played she suddenly had the feeling that something waited for her when she returned. She would only know what that was when the music finished and she had to face it. A small mark on a huge view. Perhaps it wasn't there. Perhaps it wasn't true.

They finally finished as if in a dream and stood side by side. The audience always clapped loudly, but this was louder than usual, and she could see from the look in Mark's eyes that they had played excellently. There followed calls for more, and now she could hear a hundred feet hitting the floor. Mark had tears in his eyes, but her smile was stiff now. As she sat back down and bent her head down, she did not look at her partner. She began to play the gentle notes, surprising him, but then she heard him breathe in because he knew it well. He was smiling as he sang:

In a field by the river my love and I did stand
And on my leaning shoulder she laid her snow-white hand.
She told me take life easy, as the grass grows on the weirs;
But I was young and foolish, and am now full of tears.

When they finished, the audience all stood, and there was shouting and whistling. But only Mark Berner stayed on stage. As he made a bow, he looked across at her worriedly. She was walking quickly away, her eyes on her feet. She went down the steps and hurried towards the exit.

———————

She found her coat and, not caring about the rain, walked to the apartment as quickly as she could in her high shoes. When she got there, a couple of the candles were still burning. She stood still, her hair wet and flat, and tried to remember a woman's name. So much had happened since she last thought of her. She remembered a face and heard a voice, and then it came back. *Marina Greene.* Fiona took her phone from her handbag. She apologized for calling so late at night. "Yes," Marina Greene said, "it was four weeks ago." She told her the few details she knew and said she was surprised that Fiona had not been told.

Fiona remained standing in the same place. The music she had just played was not on her mind. She had forgotten the concert. Two thoughts came into her mind. Why didn't you tell me? Why didn't you ask for my help? The answer came back in her own imagined voice. *I did.*

She turned and went to the bedroom to find the poem in her bedside table, where she had kept it. She went directly to the last

lines – God standing in the water saying that she, the fish, was
Satan and he, Adam, must pay the fine.

And God stood on the water, and He said this to me
"That fish was the voice of Satan, and you must pay the fine.
Her kiss was the kiss of Judas, her kiss sold my name.
May he

She came back to the sitting room and sat on the chaise longue,
leaning closer to the words. "Knife" had been taken out, so had
"pay", "let him", "blame" and **slain**. The word "himself" was
taken out, put in, taken out again. Yes, now she understood.

May he who drowns my cross by his own hand be slain.

When she heard the front door open, she didn't turn away,
and this was how Jack saw her as he entered the sitting room.

"You were brilliant!" he said. "Everyone loved it."

He came back with the rest of the wine and two fresh glasses.
He didn't notice how pale she was as he poured wine into hers
and gave it to her. Then, he went across the room and put the
Jarrett record back on.

She said, "Jack, not now."

"Of course, after tonight. Stupid of me."

She knew that he wanted to get back to where they were
before the concert, and she felt sorry for him. Soon he would
want to kiss her. He started talking to her about the concert, of
how proud he was of her and what all the people had said about
her after she left. She listened and said nothing. Finally, seeing
her face, he paused.

"What's wrong?"

"I'm all right."

He suddenly remembered a question he had failed to ask. "Why did you walk off stage at the end?"

"That last song. 'The Salley Gardens'. It was too much for me."

He looked like he didn't believe her. He had heard her and Mark do it many times before. "How?" he asked.

She said, "A memory. From the summer."

"Yes?" He didn't sound very interested.

"A young man played that tune to me on his violin. He was just learning. It was in a hospital. I sang with him. I think we were quite loud. Then he wanted to play it again, but I had to leave."

Jack was not in the mood to play games. She heard the confusion in his voice. "Start again. Who was this?"

"A very strange and beautiful young man." She spoke quietly. "You remember – the boy I visited in hospital. A Jehovah's Witness, very ill, refusing a transfusion. It was in the newspapers."

If he needed reminding, it was because he had been with Melanie at the time. If he hadn't been, they would have discussed the case.

"I ruled for the hospital to treat him, and he recovered. The judgment had . . . it had an effect on him. I think he had strong feelings for me."

Jack put down his empty glass. "Go on."

"When I was on circuit he followed me up to Newcastle. And I . . ." She wasn't going to tell him what happened there, and then she changed her mind. "He walked through the rain to find me and . . . I did something so stupid. I don't know what I was . . . I kissed him. I *kissed* him."

He stepped away from her, but she no longer cared.

"He was the sweetest boy. He wanted to come and live with us."

"Us?"

Jack Maye had worked in a university all his adult life. He knew that people could do and think different things at the same time, but knowing this could not protect him. She saw the anger in his face.

"He thought I could change his life. I suppose he wanted me to be his teacher. He was so hungry for life, for everything. And I didn't –"

"So you kissed him, and he wanted to live with you. What are you trying to tell me?"

"I sent him away." She shook her head, and for a moment she couldn't speak. Then she looked at Jack. He stood away from her with his feet apart and arms crossed, his face stiff with anger. She could hear the rain beating the window.

"So what happened?" he asked. "Where is he now?"

She spoke quietly. "I heard it tonight, from Runcie. Some weeks ago, his leukaemia came back, and he was taken into hospital. He refused the transfusion they wanted to give him. That was his decision. He was eighteen, and there was nothing they could do. He died."

"So he died for his faith?" Her husband's voice was cold.

"I think he killed himself."

For some seconds neither of them spoke. They heard voices, laughing and footsteps from outside in the square. People were coming home from the concert.

"Were you in love with him, Fiona?"

The question destroyed her. She let out a terrible sound, like an animal in pain. "Oh Jack, he was just a child! A boy. A lovely boy!" Then she began to cry at last, her arms hanging by her sides, while her husband watched. Jack was shocked to see his wife, who was always so self-controlled, be so deeply emotional.

She could no longer speak, and the crying would not stop. She could not bear any longer to be seen. She hurried along the corridor towards the bedroom, and the further away from him she got, the louder she cried. She reached the bedroom and, shutting the door hard behind her, fell on to the bed.

Half an hour later, when she woke, climbing up from a dream, she had no memory of falling asleep. She thought about Adam falling ill again, returning home to his loving parents, the kindly elders, returning to the faith. Or using it as the perfect cover to destroy himself. *May he who drowns my cross by his own hand be slain.* She remembered him in the Intensive Care ward, the pale thin face, the arms like poles, so ill but so determined, so full of life. Pages of his poetry on the bed, asking her to stay and play their song again.

In court she offered him, instead of death, all of life and love that lay ahead of him. And protection against his religion. Without faith, how open and beautiful and terrifying the world must have seemed to him. With that thought, she went back into a deeper sleep and woke minutes later to the sound of the rain outside. Would it ever stop? She thought of him walking towards her

Newcastle lodgings through the rain, finding a way in the dark. He must have seen the lights in the windows and known she was there. What did he want exactly? And why did he believe he could find it in a woman in her sixtieth year? A woman who had taken no risks in her life except having a few wild experiences with her cousins many years ago?

She should have been glad that he was so interested in her, and ready to listen to him and help him. Instead, she had done something which could not be forgiven. She had kissed him, then sent him away. Then ran away herself. Failed to answer his letters. Failed to understand the warning in his poem. How guilty she felt now for her worries about whether someone had seen them. Her mistake was much greater than anything her colleagues could accuse her of. Adam came looking for her, and she offered nothing in religion's place, no protection even though the Children Act was clear: his interests were the most important thing for her to worry about. How many pages, how many judgments had she written about that? *No child is an island.* She thought her work ended at the courtroom walls. But how could it? He came to find her, wanting what everyone wanted, and what only free-thinking people could give. Meaning.

She turned in the bed and was surprised to see Jack lying close to her. He reached out a hand and pushed the hair gently from her eyes. She could see his face in the light from the hall.

"I've been watching you sleep," he said.

After a long while, she whispered, "Thank you."

Then she asked him if he would still love her once she had told him the whole story. It was an impossible question for he knew almost nothing yet. She suspected he would tell her that she should not feel guilty.

He put his hand on her shoulder and pulled her to him. "Of course I will."

They lay face to face while the rain fell heavily on the city outside. And, as their marriage slowly began again, she told him in a quiet voice of her guilt, of the sweet boy's passion for life, and of her part in his death.

During-reading questions

CHAPTER FIVE

1 What does Fiona think are her real reasons for going to the hospital?
2 Why does Fiona like hospitals?
3 How does Adam behave towards Fiona when they meet?

CHAPTER SIX

1 What does Fiona decide about Adam? Why does she decide this?
2 What reasons does Jack give for leaving her to be with Melanie and then returning?
3 How does Fiona feel about Jack's return?

CHAPTER SEVEN

1 Why does Fiona feel angry towards the husbands and wives whose cases she hears?
2 How does Adam feel about the Jehovah's Witness religion now, and why have his feelings changed?
3 Why doesn't Fiona reply to the letter?

CHAPTER EIGHT

1 Why do judges go on circuit?
2 Why is Newcastle special to Fiona?
3 What is the problem that needs Fiona's immediate attention?

CHAPTER NINE

1 How did Adam find Fiona?
2 Why does Adam say that he wants to see her?
3 What does Fiona ask Pauling to do?

CHAPTER TEN

1 How does Fiona feel about the kiss afterwards?
2 What does she do to make herself feel better?
3 What happens in Jack and Fiona's relationship during this chapter?

CHAPTER ELEVEN

1 What do Fiona and Jack agree to before the concert?
2 What did Adam mean to tell Fiona in the last line of his poem?
3 How does Jack react when Fiona tells him about Adam?

After-reading questions

1 What did Sherwood Runcie tell Fiona in Chapter Eleven, do you think?
2 Should Fiona have been able to rule on Adam's case, do you think, or should he have been able to decide his own treatment?
3 Should Fiona have replied to Adam's letters, do you think? How might this have changed the end of the story?
4 Will Jack and Fiona be happy in the future, do you think? Why/Why not?
5 What kind of woman was Fiona, and did she deserve any blame for Jack leaving her, do you think?

Exercises

1 These sentences are hypothetical (Fiona does not know
for sure that they will happen). Write the sentences in
your notebook in the first person, and make them definite.

1 She would be humiliated by being left for a younger woman.
   I will be humiliated by being left for a younger woman...........................

2 She wondered if she should simply agree to anything he wanted.

3 She knew that she could be destroyed by this affair.

4 Nothing would be the same when she came away.

5 He could have done it "behind her back".

6 It would happen, with or without her permission.

7 He would leave her, and the world would go on.

8 She would have called after him, but what could she say?

CHAPTER TWO

2 These sentences use ellipsis (when words are missed out).
Write the sentences in full in your notebook.

1 First the facts.
   First, she had to look at/think about the facts.

2 No sound from the bedroom.

3 Just the traffic, and the rain.

4 Wanting it, not wanting it.

5 "Meaning?"

6 Seven weeks and a day.

7 Life, love, death and a race against time.

8 Just past ten-thirty.

3 Are these sentences *true* or *false*? Write the correct
answers in your notebook.

1 Fiona plays some piano before she leaves for
work. .... *false* ....

2 She walks past a car showroom on her way to work.

3 Fiona feels sorry for herself when she thinks about all the
kind things she has done for Jack.

4 Fiona and Jack decided to have children when they were
older.

5 Fiona became a High Court judge and then realized she
would never have children.

CHAPTER FOUR

4 Who is thinking this, do you think? Write the correct
names in your notebook.

1 "I am going to behave normally. No one will guess that I am
suffering inside." ...... *Fiona Maye* .....

2 "I must make a strong argument for the hospital to do the
blood transfusion."

3 "I talked to him about the awful death he might have."

4 "I must make my best case for the family."

5 "I know his face, but I don't think he's been in my
court before."

6 "Of course, I will feel terrible when he dies, but he must not
accept blood from another human. That is pollution."

7 "It is my job to look after this boy, and I don't want him to die."

5 **Match these words to the definitions. Write the answers in your notebook.**

Example: 1 − f

1	innocence	**a**	an organization that provides public services
2	hammer	**b**	seriously, meaning what you say
3	ward	**c**	a public service that provides a place for children to live if their parents cannot look after them safely
4	delusion	**d**	a tool for hitting things
5	authority	**e**	Many people believe that this is the part of a person that continues after they die.
6	care	**f**	when someone does not know much about life and the world, and does not do bad things
7	earnestly	**g**	a large room in a hospital containing several beds
8	soul	**h**	an idea or belief that is not true

6 **Complete these sentences with the correct form of the verb in your notebook.**

1 His faith was true and should ...._be respected_........ (**respect**).

2 "He has only .... (**know**) life as a Jehovah's Witness, and so of course he will have the strong ideas of his faith."

3 "He must .... (**protect**) from his religion and from himself, so I rule against the wishes of Adam and his parents."

4 The night before, it .... (**be**) a dark and sad thing to do, but tonight she felt light and free.

5 She unlocked the door and walked in without .... (**look**) back.

6 They both knew all the things that were .... (**not be**) said.

7 He was a bloody fool, he realized, to .... (**drive**) by sexual need.

8 She was disappointed that he .... (**not stay**) away a little longer.

7 **Match the two parts of these sentences in your notebook.**

Example: 1 – e

1 That summer, the courts seemed to be filled with lots of

a ecstasy in the statistician's bed.

2 Sometimes, the children never saw their fathers again because they

b the letter before it sounded friendly enough.

3 Fiona sometimes wanted to send them all to prison because they

c met someone.

4 Fiona did not feel better to hear that Jack had not found

d put their needs above the interests of their children.

5 Fiona wished that Jack had given her

e marriage break-ups.

6 Fiona wondered if Jack had

f more time to make a decision.

7 Fiona wrote four drafts of

g disappeared into new marriages to make new children.

8 Complete these sentences with the correct word in your notebook.

law courts	lodgings	sick
drawing room	heater	butler

1 They were nice ....*lodgings*........, with grand bedrooms and excellent cooks.

2 The idea of having a stranger's blood inside me makes me ....

3 Fiona was in Newcastle and being driven to the .... on the riverside.

4 Leadman Hall was a beautiful building. It had a .... and nine servants.

5 They had drinks in the .... before their dinner.

6 It was very cold, so the butler said he would bring them a ....

CHAPTER NINE

9 Write questions for these answers in your notebook.

1 *Why did Fiona ask Pauline to bring in a heater?*
Because Adam looked frozen.

2 He looked them up on the internet.

3 She had not noticed that they were cold and damp.

4 Because he had an argument with his father about religion.

5 Because he wanted to thank her.

6 She wrote, "All of love and life that lie ahead of him."

7 Because they did not have much room in their apartment.

8 She regretted it, but it was too late to stop what she'd started.

CHAPTER TEN

10 Put these sentences in the correct order in your notebook.

a .... Fiona decides that Adam is likely to forget her.

b .... Fiona finishes her circuit.

c .... Pauling starts driving her to Carlisle.

d .... Fiona's relationship with Jack slowly improves.

e .... Fiona calls Jack and arranges a dinner.

f .... Late October comes, and the clocks go back.

g ....*1*..... Fiona hears the rest of her cases in Newcastle.

h .... Fiona receives a poem from Adam.

CHAPTER ELEVEN

11 Correct these sentences in your notebook.

1 Fiona had not heard Keith Jarrett's *Facing You* before.
Fiona had heard Keith Jarrett's Facing You many times. Jack had introduced her to it....

2 Fiona liked the freedom of jazz.

3 Fiona drank three glasses of wine.

4 Fiona felt fine as she played the piano.

5 Fiona and Mark had planned to play "The Salley Gardens" that night.

6 Fiona and Jack had discussed the Jehovah's Witness case.

7 Jack had often seen his wife upset.

8 Jack cannot forgive Fiona when she tells him about Adam.

12 **What do these sayings from the story mean? Write your answers in your notebook.**

1 She knew that she was in the wrong. (Chapter 3, page 30)
   She knew that she was responsible for the problem....

2 on her own ground (Chapter 4, page 32)

3 I'm my own man. (Chapter 4, page 39)

4 on dangerous ground (Chapter 4, page 40)

5 on the edge of a nervous breakdown (Chapter 5, page 41)

6 have your cake and eat it (Chapter 7, page 60)

Project work

1 Imagine you are Adam. Write a diary page describing the day that Fiona visits you in hospital and the thoughts that you have afterwards.

2 Write a newspaper article about Adam's court case, the day that Fiona goes to visit him in hospital.

3 Look online, and find out more about a religion you don't know much about. Make a presentation about it.

4 Do you agree or disagree with these sentences? Write your answers.

   a Everyone should be able to decide whether to have a particular hospital treatment.

   b Open marriages are sometimes necessary.

5 It is ten years later. Imagine you are Adam, and you survived. Write a letter to Fiona describing your life.

Essay questions

- The author writes the story from Fiona's point of view, but keeps it in the third person (he/she/it). Why does he do this, do you think? (500 words)

- What kind of woman is Fiona, and what responsibility does she have, if any, for what happens to Jack and Adam and the choices they make in the story? (500 words)

- How important is "childlessness" in the story? (500 words)

An answer key for all questions and exercises can be found at **www.penguinreaders.co.uk**

Glossary

abandoned (adj.)
left alone by someone who should
have stayed with you

accusation (n.)
You make an *accusation* when you
say that someone has done
something wrong.

affair (n.)
If someone is married or has a
serious partner and they have an
affair, they regularly have sex with
a person who is not their wife,
husband, boyfriend or girlfriend.

**AIDS (Acquired Immune
Deficiency Syndrome)** (n.)
AIDS is a serious disease that is
spread through sex and blood.
It affects the body's ability to
protect itself from other diseases.

authority (n.)
an organization that provides
public services

barrister (n.)
a lawyer who works in a high court.
A lawyer prepares the *case* but a
barrister stands in front of a judge
and argues that *case* for their *client*.

bloody (adj.)
used to show that you are very
angry about what you are saying.
You say *bloody* when you *swear*.

brief (adj.)
If you are *brief*, you say something
using only a few words.

briefcase (n.)
a case for carrying papers, etc.
to work

butler (n.)
a man who works in someone's
home, welcoming guests, bringing
drinks and food, and giving
messages to people who live there

care (n.)
a public service that provides a place
for children to live if their parents
cannot look after them safely

case (n.)
In law, a *case* is a matter that is
decided by a judge. If someone
makes a *case* or proves their *case*,
they give a set of facts for or against
something. In medicine, a *case* is
an example of a particular disease
which a person has.

cell (n.)
the smallest part that all plants and
animals are made of

chaise longue (n.)
a chair with an arm on one side
and a long seat for your legs. They
are usually found in the houses of
wealthy people.

Chareidi (adj.)
Chareidi Jewish people follow the
rules of Judaism very strictly

clerk (n.)
someone who looks after documents
in a court

client (n.)
someone who pays you to do a job for them

colleague (n.)
a person who you work with

community (n.)
a group of people who are all the same in a particular way; for example, they live the same way or in the same place, or they believe the same things

conflict (n.)
a difficult situation in which you want different things at the same time

conjoined twins (n.)
two people who are born with their bodies joined together

cross-examine (v.)
A *barrister cross-examines* someone in court when they ask them difficult questions after another lawyer has asked them a first set of questions.

declaration (n.)
If you make a *declaration*, you announce something important.

defence (n.)
Your *defence* is something you say to support yourself when someone has accused you of something.

delusion (n.)
an idea or belief that is not true

depressed (adj.)
If you are *depressed*, your mood is usually very negative, and you may have *depression*. *Depression* is a mental illness. If something *depresses* you, it makes you feel *depressed*.

division (n.)
a part of an organization

draft (n. and v.)
A *draft* is a document that you have not yet finished working on. You *draft* a document when you write it.

drawing room (n.)
a room in a big house where guests are offered drinks, etc.

drug (n.)
a chemical that is used as a medicine

earnestly (adv.)
seriously, meaning what you say

ecstasy (n.)
a feeling of pleasure and excitement

elder (n.)
an older member of a religious group who gives advice and makes decisions

evidence (n.)
things that make you believe that something is true

exist (v.)
If something *exists*, people can see or experience it in the real world.

faith (n.)
someone's *faith* is their religion

faithful (adj.)
If you are *faithful* to your romantic partner, you do not have *affairs*.

freedom (n.)
being free to live as you want and not being controlled by someone

Hague Convention (n.)
an international agreement that makes it possible to bring back a child who has been illegally taken to another country by one of their parents

hammer (n.)
a tool for hitting things

heaven (n.)
Many people believe that, if you are a good person, you will go to *heaven* when you die.

humiliated (adj.)
very embarrassed and worried about what other people will think of you, usually because of something that another person has done to you

idiot (n.)
a stupid person

innocence (n.)
when someone does not know much about life and the world, and does not do bad things

Intensive Care (n.)
part of a hospital for patients who are very ill or badly injured

interests (n.)
someone's *interests* are what is best for them rather than for someone else

Jewish (adj.)
used to describe a person whose religion is Judaism. The first *Jewish* people lived in Israel, but now they live in many places all over the world.

Judas (n.)
someone who hurts a friend by breaking a promise. In the Bible, Judas Iscariot was a man who broke a promise he had made to Jesus.

judgment (n.)
in a court, a decision made by a judge

justice (n.)
the way in which judges decide whether to punish people, for example, by sending them to prison. The *Royal Courts of Justice* is an important place where judges decide on how to punish people for serious crimes. The *Lord Chief Justice* is the most important person working in English law.

lean (v.)
to move the top part of your body so that it is closer to something

leukaemia (n.)
a type of cancer that affects the blood. (Cancer is a serious illness that makes *cells* grow in a way that is not normal.)

lodgings (n.)
a room or a house where you pay to live while you are visiting a place

obsessed (adj.)
If you are *obsessed* with something, you think about it and worry about it all the time.

operation (n.)
When a doctor does an *operation*, they cut a person's body and repair it or take something out.

passion (n.); **passionate** (adj.)
Passion is a very strong feeling such as love or anger. A *passionate* person often experiences *passion*.

permission (n.)
If you give someone *permission* to do something, you allow or permit them to do it.

piece (n.)
A *piece* of music is music that has been created. You play or sing it.

professor (n.)
an important teacher at a university

reasonable (adj.);
reasonableness (n.)
A *reasonable* person behaves in a sensible and fair way. *Reasonableness* is behaving in this way.

residence (n.)
Residence is where someone lives.

risk (n.)
the chance that something bad might happen

Satan (n.); **satanic abuse** (n.)
Satan is another name for the devil (= in many religions, the strongest bad power). *Satanic abuse* is cruel or violent behaviour against someone involving the worship of (= religious love for) *Satan*.

self-pity (n.)
a feeling of sadness about your situation, thinking that other people should feel sorry for you

sexual (adj.)
Sexual means connected to sex.

sick (adj.)
You are *sick* when food from your stomach comes out of your mouth. If something makes you *sick*, it makes this happen.

slain (v.)
Slain is the past participle of the verb *slay*. *Slay* is an old word that means to kill in a violent way.

social worker (n.)
a person whose job is to help and
advise people who have
social problems

soul (n.)
Many people believe that the *soul* is
the part of a person that continues
after they die.

spare (adj.)
A *spare* room or a *spare* bed is a room
or bed that you can allow someone
to use because you do not need it.

statistician (n.)
someone whose job is to work
with numbers

submission (n.)
a document that you give to
someone who will make a decision
about it

summarize (v.)
to give the most important facts
about something

swear in (phr. v.)
If someone *swears* you *in*, or if you
are *sworn in*, you make a formal
promise in court.

sworn (v.)
Sworn is the past participle of *swear*.
If you *swear*, you use rude words,
often because you are angry.
The past form is *swore*.

threaten (v.); **threat** (n.)
If a person *threatens* you, they
make you think that they will do
something bad to you if you do
not do what they want. They make
a *threat*.

thrill (n.)
a very strong feeling of excitement

Torah (n.)
the written beliefs and laws of the
Jewish religion

transfusion (n.); **transfused** (v.)
A blood *transfusion* is when blood
from another person is put into
someone's body. If someone is
transfused, they receive blood from
someone else's body.

ward (n.)
a large room in a hospital containing
several beds

whisky (n.)
a strong light-brown drink. *Whisky* is
alcohol.